The Barbarian's Warrior Bride

by

Kay Jeffery

Nuns and Barbarians

The Barbarian's Warrior Bride

Cover Art by *Teddi Black*

The Wild Rose Press, Inc.
PO Box 708
Adams Basin, NY 14410-0708
Visit us at www.thewildrosepress.com

Publishing History
First Edition, 2026
Trade Paperback Print ISBN 978-1-5092-6466-7
Digital ISBN 978-1-5092-6467-4

Nuns and Barbarians
Published in the United States of America

Dedication

To my own white knight:
Thank you for championing me through thick and thin
. . . and making me laugh along the way.
You're the greatest. Silly songs included.

Come away to an enchanted island somewhere in the Atlantic, hidden in the primordial mist, an island where women a long time ago and over many years sought refuge from a world forged against them. The first to arrive found all she could have wanted: shelter, food, beauty, safety, magic, and eventually, as others arrived, companionship. Together they built a sisterhood. In the gentle hands of a benevolent spirit, the island nurtured the refugees, and in return the sisters served the island as the nuns of Adytum Abbey. There they lived and worked and created and led and thrived. They regained themselves. That is, until one day ...

Chapter 1

The Present: Sometime around 1000 years ago

There was something on the wind.

Sister Mary Irmengard squinted into the distance, across the gently undulating sea. But against the dark dawn sky, only just beginning to tint a golden yellow with the coming day, she could see nothing.

At least, not yet.

She breathed out a slow, measured stream of air.

She would wait.

Inhaling the cool, salty breeze, she turned all of her senses toward the rising sun, away from Adytum Abbey. The wind was blowing from the east, bringing with it…she knew not what. Something foreign, something other. The convent on Adytum had served as her refuge for the last fifteen years, as it had for the other women of the island. They were her family. This was their home. Irma would allow no one to breach it.

Even if she had to kill to protect it.

Even if she was killed in its defense.

Irma folded her arms over the closely woven vest of the battle gear that covered her generous bosom. Conscious of her sword's weight in the sheath that hung from her belt, over her widely curving hip, she drew in another careful breath. A frosty determination filled her. She waited, steady and sure, as the sun rose over the mobile sea.

When the longboats finally appeared on the horizon, lit in silhouette by the bright sliver of sun bringing in the day, they were as of yet still tiny in the distance. Irma uncrossed her arms, remaining cool and determined. Gone were the days when temper fueled her, when she could be brought to an uncontrolled, murderous rage. Her duty today would be performed with the cold, harsh detachment required to maintain focus on her one mission: Protect the Abbey.

She rested one hand on her sword. With the other, she raised the signal to her fellow guardians. They would meet these invaders head-on.

And hope the island's spirit would give them strength for what was to come.

Her home, her family, would be safe…if it was the last thing she ever did.

Thus, when the barbarians first spied the white walls of the convent as it emerged from the dawn mist, they would also see the glint of sunlight on the raised swords of the island's Amazonian warriors. At the center of their formation shone the fiery halo of the woman who stood as their general, leather clad and unflinching. Ready to do battle.

****

Fifteen Years Earlier

With a howl of fury, Yrse hurled the barrel at the man she'd loved. The man for whom she'd abandoned everything she had, everything she knew, everything she *was.*

"Bastard!" she yelled through bared teeth. "Faithless swine! Hedge-born loiter-sack! Dung-eating coxcomb!" A chair flew through the air this time as the coxcomb in question ducked in the corner of the public house, arms over his head.

"What—Yrse?" The loiter-sack's voice rose in incredulity. "What are you—?" His question ended in a yelp as he dodged a succession of flagons flying at him.

She roared again, this time in frustration. *By Thor's hairy bacraut, why was he still standing?* Foolish tears obstructed her aim. She dashed them from her eyes with violent finger strokes and then grabbed the next available object, so she could strike true this time. *Good, a knife.* Finally, a weapon that would make him bleed, just as her heart was bleeding in agony at his betrayal.

Fire blazing from her eyes, Yrse raised her hand to throw the knife—only to have her wrist clasped in a large, meaty fist.

Growling with rage, she neatly twisted from this man's grasp, leveling the knife at him now. "Don't. Touch. Me." She snarled and lunged at him with her weapon, but then whirled to throw it at that faithless swine who was creeping out of his corner. The knife thunked just inches from his hip, failing to unman him, curse the gods.

Swallowing his yelp, the cur held out his hands, those beautiful hands that had glided over her body those many months ago, that had softened her heart. *Oh, now he wheedles.* Her thoughts were cynical; she knew this move well.

"Yrse, sweetling, dearheart—" Svend started, taking a step toward her. It was another injury to hear again those words, those honeyed words she'd thought were only for her, that she had moments ago heard him using with the tavern whore outside against the building, his pants around his knees.

The scales had fallen from her eyes. Svend was handsome with his blond hair, blue eyes known for a mischievous twinkle, and well-formed limbs. But he was attractive in a boyish, small-chinned, weak, and *faithless* way, she could see now, the miserable cur.

She interrupted his sweet talk with another roar through her teeth. "Do. Not. *Charm*. Me."

Though it was now filled with men from the two bands of warriors who had come to observe the fracas, silence fell on the room.

"I saw you. Just now. With that woman." Yrse stuttered as the image returned vividly to her mind's eye. "You were …" She choked at the image of him entwined with the tavern wench.

"Yrse, she's no one! It's just the heat of battle, you know? You are my darling, my love, my *saeta* …"

She drew in a pained gasp, tight with the constricting bindings she wore around her chest. This man would pay for what he had done to her. He would pay, and he would hurt. "How dare you use those words with me after what I just saw."

"Signus." A low voice sounded from behind her.

"Back off." She tossed the command over her shoulder, wiping hands wet with idiotic tears on her leather trousers.

Her eyes darted around the small inn's public room again, and she grabbed a wooden bowl to throw at Svend's head for emphasis. Crowing in satisfaction when it hit its mark this time, only wishing it could do more damage, Yrse cast her eyes around for an object more potentially lethal to heft at him when he tried his next plea for mercy. She was frustrated to see only some spoons left on the large table that stood between her and the carrion-eating *kuensami*. The table itself? Too heavy, she reckoned.

"Yrse, darling—I'm sorry! I'm sorry!" he shouted when she made like she'd fling herself bodily over the table at him. "But how are you even here? I didn't even recognize you. I mean, look at you!" He gestured toward her body with shaking hands. "How was I to know—"

Yrse knew what he saw; she had worked carefully to achieve the effect. She looked like a man, a warrior. Like the rest of the band.

The sides of her head she kept shaved bare two inches above her ears and around the back. Each morning she braided the flame-red hair at her crown down the center until it dangled in a fiery rope to the base of her neck. She'd wrapped a long piece of linen several times around her torso to squash her generous breasts closer to her chest and wore her tunic loosely tucked into her leather trousers. To disguise the curve of her hips, she wore a large belt that held the sheath for her sword and several smaller weapons, which she, *curse Odin's beard*, had left behind her once she had heard Svend's band was in this village. That she had finally caught up to him.

She had had no thought but to see him, having imagined the moment so many times in her girlish fantasies. She had not wanted to look like a man for him but like a woman—a woman worthy of him.

No more. Now she saw he was not worthy of her and never had been.

Pocketing the spoons, Yrse eased around the edge of the table, toward where the straggle-bearded goat cowered in the corner. Nothing was between them now.

"How were you to know that I would follow you?

That I would take up the mantle of warrior and fight your battles with you—better than you, as they can testify." She waved her hand at the wall of warriors who stood behind her. "How were you to know *that I would witness your faithlessness with my own eyes?*"

Though she spoke in controlled tones, they vibrated with menace, her eyes blazed, and she could tell he knew he was far from safe. One of Svend's hands reached for the knife protruding from the wall in the vain hope of arming himself with it, but it was too deeply buried. *Like the knife in my heart*, Yrse thought, anger spiking again as the pain of betrayal surged through her.

"How could you know I'd follow you to the ends of the earth? Because *I told you I would*, you filthy, serpent-tongued, pox-ridden, small-pricked oathbreaker! And unlike you, I keep my word."

With that, she feinted to his left and then lunged to intercept him on the right when he tried to run away. *Gutless turd.* With a mighty bellow, she tackled her erstwhile love to the grimy dirt floor and stabbed him repeatedly with the pointed handle of one of the wooden spoons, in the gut, then the groin, determined to unman him.

She was going for his eyes next when large hands hauled her off the screaming knave. Yrse sent her sharp elbow back into this man's midsection, which he took with a bitten-off curse. But he succeeded in wrapping her in massive arms that constrained her punches. Yrse managed to land one more good kick to Svend's balls before the man who'd grabbed her lifted her away entirely. Though frustrated at the interruption, Yrse knew some satisfaction when Svend remained curled up on the floor, holding his privates and whimpering.

Even as she witnessed her former lover's pain with a measure of gratification, she was surprised that the man who'd restrained her was carrying her with ease outside the tavern. No lightweight, she stood as tall as many of the men with whom she served in her crew. The outside air hitting her tear-wet face had a bracing effect, and the full realization of what she had done—and what would inevitably follow next—spread through her in an icy wave. She was a woman among men; she had pretended to be one of them for months, but she had lied.

She did not dare look them in the eyes. Who knew what they would do to her?

And so, as soon as the man released her, she took to her feet, running as fast as she could away from the inn, from the band of warriors she'd thought of as her comrades, from this whole miserable village. The painful realization that life as she knew it was yet again over roared in her ears like the turbulent ocean.

As a result, she didn't hear the man who'd taken her from the inn say, either to himself or to the others who'd come out, "Now there's a shame. A fine warrior, that one was. Much too fine for that milksop in there."

Chapter 2

The Present

The clank of swords colliding, the smack of bodies as they plowed into each other, and the grunts and yells of violence echoed off the walls of the Abbey's courtyard, which had become a battlefield. Blinking the sweat from her eyes, Sister Mary Irmengard spared a glance for her fellow guardians as they defended their keep against the barbarians.

The other women, though streaked with mud and goddess knew what else, appeared to be on their feet. That was not to say they were faring well.

Indeed, they all seemed to be losing ground. Though they had begun the fight close to the courtyard gate, their stance had fallen back ever closer to the high white walls of Adytum Abbey itself.

It should never have come to this. On no account should the invaders have been able to breach the courtyard enclosure. Not only was there strong magic along the edges of the convent walls, but Irma had also sent two of her best archers, Sister Agatha and Sister Veronique, to hold off the men as they came up from the shore along the narrow path bordered by barbed vines.

The two frontline guardians had vanished, the men had scaled the courtyard walls, and Irma feared the worst.

At present, the Abbey's main entrance lay directly behind her. Two men faced her, swords drawn. They were breathing hard, at least, and knew their victory was not assured. Their frustration at how slowly they were advancing on the Abbey gave Irma a small shot of satisfaction, and she bared her teeth at them in defiance. She was acutely aware that she was the only force standing in the way of these two men gaining entrance to the convent.

For more than a dozen years, the spirit of the island had given the convent's residents every advantage. Although external challenges had been rare, the guardians had met them fiercely and decisively. She had sensed the goddess firmly on their side. They were protected by a divine presence Irma did not understand but believed in, respected, trusted.

But as the break of dawn drew toward midmorning, Irma had developed an unsettled feeling in her gut. A warrior in her previous life, she knew the soldier's instinct for good fortune or bad. This was like nothing she'd experienced. The steadiness of her feet in the dark mud of the courtyard reminded her of the goddess's support and strength. That remained. Persisted.

And yet, her blows did not seem to land. Her sword had drawn no blood this morning.

Irma had the uneasy thought that the goddess might be protecting the men, too.

Hastily, she discarded the unwanted idea and focused on the two barbarians in front of her, one shorter than she and the other substantially taller. *Minimus and Maximus*, she mentally labeled them with a smirk. Their size difference could have been a disadvantage, with her facing off against swords raised at varying heights, but

Irma knew her craft. When Minimus lunged, she deflected his blow and allowed the force of motion to carry her blade over her shoulder, circling around the side to block Maximus's strike.

Yet Maximus had not done the expected. He had not raised his sword while hers was engaged with his partner and she was most vulnerable. Instead, he retained his stance, peering at her through squinted eyes while her sword sliced harmlessly through the air in front of him. Minimus appeared to be bracing himself to engage with her again, but the taller one barked harsh words to him, and he paused, sword pulled back, and looked at his comrade, baffled. When the shorter one replied, Maximus repeated his earlier command.

Irma stood back, feet apart in the muddy soil, sword raised in both hands, ready to strike while Minimus turned to his partner, and the two men engaged in a muffled, though quite heated, argument.

By the goddess, what oafs! To lose their focus in battle was a deadly error. The brief urge to sweep both men's feet from beneath them took her over for a moment before she rejected it. It was another error to intrude on an argument between two armed men when one did not know the source of the disagreement.

To save her strength, she lowered her sword. Casting her eyes vigilantly around the courtyard, she saw disorder everywhere. It occurred to her again that, though covered in dirt and sweat, there was surprisingly little blood—perhaps no blood at all, in fact. Her brow lowered in a deep frown as she realized that it didn't even smell like a battlefield—no iron-rich stench of blood nor the other horrific smells of wounded flesh and deathly fear she remembered from battles past.

What was this then?

In frustration, she turned back around to the men just as Minimus shoved Maximus, and they both fell back.

Enough.

"Raise your swords, arrogant barbarian swine, and feel *the wrath of the goddess!*" she yelled, inviting an offensive attack. Though her words were hot, her will was cold as ice.

To her disbelief, Minimus threw up his hands and backed away. When her eyes darted to Maximus, narrowing on him with a glare, he spread his hands to the side, leaving himself vulnerable to her sword.

Thrown off, Irma lowered her sword again. "You miserable brutish cur," she taunted, using words as her weapons. "Too cowardly to charge against even a mere woman?" She sneered at him.

Absurdly, Maximus bowed to her. "You have bested us, fair warrior," he said in a language she was shocked to recognize. A language from a past she tried not to remember. "My companion and I yield to your superior skill …and passion."

Was that a twinkle in his eye? Did his gaze linger on her form, here and there, with—by the goddess, was that *lust*?

Irma's vision shaded to red. She could feel the heat of temper, tamped down deep for so many years, rising within her, explosive. A cry of rage swelled up from her feet through her core, propelled by her lungs into the air between her and her foes. Dropping her sword, she launched herself bodily at the large bear of a man.

Surprised, he failed utterly to defend himself. She crashed headlong into his body, bearing him down into the wet dirt of the courtyard. Her fingers grasped the dagger at her belt. But as she drew it to gut the disrespectful lummox, he displayed quick reflexes, newly engaged, and clasped her wrist, pinching it such that the small blade fell uselessly to the side. With her other hand, she landed a fist to his gut that had him exhaling a pained grunt, but then he'd rolled them over so that she was beneath him in the mud. Grabbing a fistful of the wet ground, she slapped the muck over his eyes and forehead, satisfied when she heard him cursing, and then slammed her other fist into his stubborn jaw.

Tossing his shaggy head, he shook off the blow. "By Thor's hammer, you're a pugnacious lass!" Strangely, it sounded—almost—complimentary. Irma took the advantage to hoist up his leg, unbalancing him, and flipped them both over.

The two of them rolled over each other in the mud. First him on top, then her, then him again. Both gasping for air, they paused.

Their eyes met for an electric moment.

Both of them burst out laughing.

Irma laughed up into this man's muddy, smiling visage until tears streaked down her cheeks and her sides hurt. When her laughter subsided, she inhaled steadily, looked up at the cloud-strewn sky, and glanced back at him—bursting into mirth again at the sight of his face. "You, you," she stuttered between gasping breaths. "The mud. You've got …a badger's mask!" She broke into loud, lusty merriment again, aware of his booming guffaws joining hers.

"You should see …yourself!" he managed. "Mud here." He drew a finger down her nose. "And here." He touched her cheeks, one and then the other. "And here." He tapped the point of her chin. "Like a painted doll!"

"I'll—show you—a—painted …doll!" She laughed up at him, twisting her body beneath his and turning them over again in the mud. She lifted her hand to touch him, but as her finger traced the curve of his smiling cheek, and she wriggled atop his strong, hard body, she felt the laughter drain from her, leaving behind …

Her eyelids sank to half-mast.

Her aggressive decisiveness, so valuable to her in combat, suddenly impelled her to change the nature of their duel. Keeping her eyes on his, she slowly lowered her head and then, with a quick movement, bit his plump lower lip, holding it with just enough pressure to show him she could have drawn blood, without actually doing so.

His pupils flared within hazel irises. That meaty hand of his glided firmly up her side to her back, leaving a trail of warmth, and then grabbed her head, driving his fingers into the hair at the base of her braid.

A shudder traveled down from that spot through her whole body. She shifted atop him, angling her soft curves into his hardening muscles. He emitted a long groan, and his eyelids drifted downward.

Almost simultaneously, she released his lip and he pulled her head toward him. Their mouths crushed together in a bruising kiss. When they opened to each other, their teeth briefly clashed before the kiss became all lips and tongues. As they engaged in an erotic version of swordplay, Irma struggled to align their bodies to assuage the building pressure at the juncture of her thighs. Her leather armor stretched too tightly against her swelling breasts. Every part of her wanted to rub up against every part of him.

She wanted him, skin to skin.

Her whole body was aflame, on fire for this man with the big, warm hands and the mischievous hazel eyes and the booming laugh. This man who was every bit her match in battle and, it seemed, in lust as well. For so many years, she had subjected the native passion of her spirit to the control of her rational mind and the discipline of a soldier's body, but this man had shattered that control.

She was all passion, all want, all need.

When she straddled him, opening her strong legs around the core of his body, he bent one of his legs so that his knee rose to the vulnerable apex of her thighs. He applied no pressure but used clenching hands on her hips to urge her into position, encouraging her to use the bone of his kneecap to pleasure herself. At the first touch of her tender core to his knee, she jolted. *It had been so long.*

Her body took over and she ground down on him, first cautiously, then with more pressure, grinding and rubbing until a wave of heat and light swelled up from that point to the place where their lips still pulled at each other, and she moaned heavily into his mouth. She lifted her head to pant through the rest of her orgasm, gazing again into eyes, intense and knowing. No humor in them now but another expression she could not quite identify.

Suddenly, she was on her back on the ground, his body looming over hers, blocking out the midmorning sun and covering her in shadow. She no longer had a thought for where she was. Those eyes glittered as he shifted his hands from her hips to her buttocks, lifting her center up toward the thick muscle that bulged from his leather trousers. He moved them together in one, long sensual stroke, and Irma cried out involuntarily. The wet warmth of her desire pooled toward the spot where their bodies connected, and he moved them again. The next time, she moved herself against him, urging him to a faster pace, and he grunted above her, nostrils flaring as he took in more of the air scented with their combined passion.

They moved together in what was not a battle but a dance, pressing against each other, rubbing back and forth, and then around and around, as Irma angled his leather-covered cock toward the pulsing need at her center. She used muddy hands to clutch at his broad, linen-clad shoulders as she moved beneath him, and then slid one hand down to his muscular ass to press him more tightly to her. Their movements became shorter, wedged closely together as they were, and then suddenly he bellowed out the pleasure of his release. The sound, the knowledge of having mastered him in this realm, sent Irma up in flames again, and she clutched his head to bring their mouths together once more, so they kissed and breathed into each other while they came down from their blissful peak.

Kisses turned into sweeter nuzzlings, and she realized he was murmuring things into her cheek, her neck, that she didn't quite understand. Driving the fingers of both hands into the thick, tousled brown hair at the sides of his head, Irma pulled him up. Looked into his eyes.

He grinned.

Then she grinned.

And they were laughing again, this time in sheer joy of having come together in this unexpected moment of physical bliss.

"By the god, you are the perfect woman. A goddess

in your own right!"

"You are indeed blessed this day." She laughed up at him.

"A blessed day for a wedding, at that."

"A wedding! Goddess forfend, you move quickly." Irma pushed hard against his chest so that she tumbled atop him again.

"I must be yours, sweet warrior," her Maximus said in that rumbly voice of his. "Claim me!" Laughter danced in his eyes, but she also saw clear intent. He wanted her still.

"Well, then, perhaps you do belong to me," Irma found herself replying, feeling a smug, possessive smile curve her lips. She narrowed her gaze as a thought came to her. "Are you free?" Her tone was even, yet deadly. Irma braced her forearm against his exposed neck. "Do not think to lie to me." Bitter experience had taught her to see through a man's lies.

His own expression sobered. "I am free these last six summers." A flash of some emotion—grief? regret? guilt?—passed across the mossy green-brown of his eyes, just for an instant. Then his gaze sharpened again with lusty intent. "But my beautiful Sigyn, goddess of victory, as you can see"—he gestured to himself, prone beneath her—"I am free no longer. I am your devoted captive. And I shall remain so …if you want me." He looked at her from under half-closed lids, deceptively sleepy and docile.

Though he played the prisoner, Irma did not fail to notice his thick hand slowly advancing up her thigh. Leveling a playfully severe look at her so-called captive, she grabbed that hand in hers and slammed it onto the damp ground beside his head. She leaned over him, nipped his lower lip—by the goddess, what was it about that lip?—and lowered her forehead to his.

When she pulled in a centering breath, she drew his scent into her lungs. Without conscious thought, she rubbed her smooth cheek against his, feeling the pleasant scratch of his beard, the warmth of his skin on hers. A curious sensation stole through her. It was not an instant snap of realization, but rather a slow slide downward, down, down to this man she recognized in her very bones. This man she lay atop with no fear or quarrel or even uncertainty, but instead a sense of the rightness at the two of them linked together.

She accepted it, welcomed it, and decided.

Swiftly, she pushed herself off of him and rose to her feet. "Well, then, if it's to be a wedding, there is much to do." She turned her back on him, hips swaying as she walked toward the Abbey whose main door stood fractured and open on its hinges. Before she could find anything to be alarmed at in that previously unthinkable breach, a loud war whoop pierced the air, and she was swept into the burly arms of her would-be bridegroom.

Later she would be amazed that she, Sister Mary Irmengard, coolly controlled guardian of Adytum Abbey, whose feet had never left the ground these last fifteen years, had been cuddled up bridal style without any resistance or irritation. In fact, being swept off her feet flooded her with what could only be called ...joy.

In that moment, Irma twined her arms around the neck of Maximus the Barbarian and allowed him to carry her, his warrior bride, through the doors and into the heart of the convent.

Chapter 3

When was the last time he'd held a woman thusly in his arms? Too long ago. Likely never. Not even his late wife, who'd been delicate and needed a careful touch, not even she had he held aloft in his arms. Much less had he ever experienced such a dramatic, violent, sexual battle as the lovemaking he'd shared just now with this warrior goddess—the deliverer of victory indeed.

Had he won this battle? He was about to breach the convent, as had been their aim, but somehow that mission meant little to him in this moment. Holding this woman in his arms, that was its own victory, a more important one by far.

This woman, with her blazing hair, sharp eyes, and ferocious power, was triumph.

And he knew her. He knew this woman's strength, her loyalty, and her incisive intelligence. He knew her warrior's heart. He also knew that beneath her armor lay a tender spirit and an enormous capacity for erotic, not just martial, passion.

Understanding her as he did, he realized that if he gave her too much time to think, she would shield herself again in her warrior's armor. He wanted her tender, laughing, and so invulnerable she would lay herself bare to him, confident in herself and in him. Some magic had made that vibrant inner core accessible to him, and he intended to keep it. He wanted to bind her to him before she realized who he was.

He was both brute and strategist enough to use her current ignorance to his advantage.

So, as he walked to the massive wooden doors that had been forced open sometime during their battle, he bent to murmur in her ear. "Let us consummate our nuptials, dear Sigyn. I swear I cannot wait to worship you with my body." He felt the shiver that skipped through her voluptuous form. Her arms tightened around his neck.

"Was a muddy tussle not consummation enough, Maximus?" she said with an arched look. By the gods, that low and sultry voice shook him to the core.

"Maximus, you say!" He smiled broadly at the unintended compliment. When her cheeks bloomed red, he knew she'd revealed thoughts she'd meant to keep to herself. "I'll show you that I can live up to your pet name for me, lass. But the ground is no place for wedding rites. Bring me a bed!" His bellow rang out across the courtyard.

"I should have called you a thieving badger, you filthy hulk." She laughed lustily, pointing a finger at his mud-covered face.

"Now doesn't that remind me of a tune." After a moment's reflection, Bjorn launched into an earthy ditty from his childhood. Changing the words for the moment, he sang out in a deep bass:

A spring day's dawning
Made the day
When the filthy badger
Came out to play
With lady rosy

Among the posies
Whose beauty shone like the radiant sun.

With a delighted laugh, his lady rosy joined him in a mellow contralto:

His lass was bonnie,
Guarded well,
But the badger found
Her secret bell
His mask should hide him
But the fair maid spied him
And kissed his nose with the bud of her rose.

Their strong, well-matched voices twined together harmoniously in the bawdy song. As the notes trailed off, his fair maid cackled merrily at the racy tune.

Bjorn paused momentarily at the threshold of the door that had obviously been beaten down sometime while he and his armful had waged their intimate battle. Deliberately, he placed his feet on the stone of the great hall's foyer. It was not lost on him that he had gained entry into the massive white building that had risen up out of the morning mist as their boats had approached this strange island's shore. *By Mimir's head.* He could never have guessed, even at the last dawn, that this voyage would lead him here, to the woman who had never fully left his mind, even after all these years. He did not doubt this was some divine plan the gods had for him. And he did not intend to waste this chance.

As the echo of their harmony faded, Bjorn shouted, "A bed! A bed for my bride!"

The woman in his arms laughed and punched him

hard in the arm. "Up the stairs and to the left, you oaf!" The warmth he heard in her voice demanded a response, so he captured her lips with his, groaning into her mouth.

She pulled away with a loud smack of their lips and ordered, "Take me to bed, then, my brawny swain! And be quick about it." Her fingers spiked through his hair, grabbing a fistful of it and pulling as if he were her beast of burden.

Praise Odin, he would bear this woman to the ends of the earth, if needs must, and if they were not already there.

"Woman, you have my reins, then. Guide me." He strode to the curving stone staircase at the end of the great hall.

"Oh, you need to be guided into place? Perhaps I need a more experienced lover, then, who knows where he's going."

"By Freya's cat-drawn chariot, you seek to unman me, wench! I know well how sword slides best into scabbard, and when we get to this promised chamber, I'll prove it to you." He was rewarded when she threw her head back in a loud, boisterous guffaw. He vowed he would keep that spark in her jewel-green eyes.

At the top of the steps, unwinded, he turned left toward a hallway lined by doors, some closed and some opened, through which a variety of noises issued: conversations, shouts, erotic moans, and even the rhythmic thumping of others engaged in rites of bliss. Bjorn ignored it all, striding down the hall until they reached the end where a yank on his hair pulled him back.

His soon-to-be bride—*it would be so*—reached down to grab the door handle of the very last chamber and pushed it open, revealing a small, bright-white room with no adornment that his quick glimpse could discern. Looking down at her mud-decorated face, Bjorn barked out a frustrated laugh.

"My dainty *brúðr*," he said, naming her his bride in their native language. "Between the two of us, we will utterly befoul this pristine chamber."

He could see she toyed with the idea of simply decorating the chamber with the evidence of their earlier battle. At last she discarded it with a long sigh that ended in a growl.

"Better set me down, then, Maximus, and let us to the baths." She took her hand out of his hair, and he lowered her feet to the floor. "There's a hot spring hidden among the island's cliffs."

Suddenly worried she might bolt, though he wasn't sure why, he grabbed her calloused hands in his and bent to kiss her, tilting her head back and thrusting his tongue into her sweetly open mouth as if to remind her of their mutual aim. When she started to walk backwards, he followed her like a faithful dog on a leash. Her back hit the wall, and he pressed his body against her softness, hitching her against the hard ridge of his desire. A flash of memory made him think this was not the way to have this woman, up against a wall as they were, and he pulled his head back to look at her flushed cheeks.

Seemingly unaware of what caused his retreat—perhaps she did not recall that day more than a dozen years ago?—she leaned up to take his lips again. "Not the baths, then," she murmured. "Too far." She said the words against his mouth, between little kissing bites of his lower lip. "But there's a small chamber just here." She slid out from under his body to move down a short corridor perpendicular to the long hallway, towing him behind her by the hand. At the very end, she opened another door, peered in, and tugged him in behind her. She closed the door with a sharp snap, and then splayed herself against it, as if daring him to try to escape from her.

This woman! Fire fueled his blood at her sexual confidence, and he moved toward her.

"Ah-ah!" She reproved him with a raised brow. She held up a hand to stop him and then gestured to his form, reminding him that he was covered with dirt. She was, too, of course, but he almost didn't see it, so brightly luminous did she shine through it.

This room, too, was painted a blinding white, he realized, but there were basins and tubs and linens folded into tidy stacks. Instead of wooden planks, the floor was lined with stone tiles and a long, soft carpet lay beside the largest bathing tub. A pleasantly floral smell freshened the air. The strong sun, reaching toward the sky's apex, beamed through two narrow windows, washing the whole room with bright light. Indeed, he felt at the dawn of his life, a life brand new.

Bjorn held his ground as his Sigyn moved slowly toward him, took a towel off the stack slightly behind him, and dunked it into an adjacent basin filled with the sweet-smelling water. Her body stayed an electric half inch away from his. He could feel the hairs of his arms and chest lifting at the taunting near contact.

Carefully, she took the wet cloth to his face and, with a firm touch, she began to wash him. Her eyes focused on her task, rubbing at his sun-warmed forehead, the skin around his eyes. She rinsed the cloth from where she stood and returned to wash the muck from the bridge of his nose, his cheeks. She did this again and again, deliberate strokes that instead of cooling him built a fire in him beyond what he had ever known.

As she removed his badger's mask, Bjorn experienced another stab of worry. Would she recognize him? But her bright eyes remained clear as she looked at him, now free from the battle disguise she had given him. Her eyes crinkled at the corners, and he drew a relieved breath.

She was pleased with him.

Her hands tugged his shirt from his belt, lifted it over his head, and then she bathed his neck and collarbones. Next, his torso, though the dirt had not penetrated his clothing. He saw this for the erotic dance it was. Her touch stayed firm atop the bathing cloth as she drew it down the center of his chest, across each pectoral muscle, circling each rounded bulge until he could bear it no longer.

"Now you, my vaunted Valkyrie," he murmured, taking the cloth from her hands.

"Do you admit yourself defeated in battle, then?" Her taunt was playful.

"That I do." He kept a straight face, hoping she could hear the bone-deep seriousness of his admission. It was no concession but rather a vow, one drawn from his very core.

Rinsing the cloth in the fragrant water, he tenderly dabbed at the mess he'd made of her, removing the dirty smudges on her cheeks, nose, chin, and that broad, noble forehead. By the nine realms, she was a beauty. Strong features framed those radiant eyes; rosy cheeks hinted at her passionate heart. With gentle strokes, he unveiled her to his gaze again, then dragged the cloth down her white, slender neck. Keeping his eyes on hers, he moved the fabric, warm from his hand now, over the generous swell of her bosom, and watched her eyelids drift downwards. He knew this submission for the voluntary gift that it was. She was still the conqueror here.

Moving forward, Bjorn inhaled deeply of the sweet scent of her swanlike throat, flicked out his tongue to trace the delicate flesh. For a moment, he allowed his eyes to take in the sight of her curving breasts above her warrior's bodice. He didn't even realize he had dropped the cloth to clutch her hips to his until she spoke.

"Not yet," she whispered.

He pulled back, a question in his eyes.

With a small shake of her head, she pointed him toward a large, white bathing vessel behind him. With the pull of a lever, she filled the tub with more of the perfumed water without releasing his gaze, his hazel eyes to her emerald. The sound of the softly flowing water seemed to draw out the lubricious intimacy of their stare. Seconds passed in rhythm with the heavy throb of his pulse, each beat ratcheting up his desire, until she pushed the lever back into place.

Stepping away from him, she struck a pose, arms out, then reached behind her to unhook the leather garment that hugged those magnificent breasts. Bjorn hardly dared to blink as the material gradually slackened until, bringing her arms back around to the front, his bride wiggled her martial dress downward, downward, revealing the large creamy orbs, topped with tight, dark-pink nipples that bobbed slightly with her movements. His gaze captured, he hardly noticed her removing her sword-belt, boots, and leather trousers, until she stood gloriously naked before him. Bjorn's eyes took in the delectable roundness of her, from breasts to hips to calves, then returned to the bright triangle of curling hair at the apex of her thighs. He caught himself on the wall to keep from falling to his knees.

Hands on her widely curving hips, she raised one winged eyebrow at him. With quick movements, he divested himself of his own boots and trousers until he stood proudly before her, his aching manhood jutting forward with clear intent. He was pleased to see that her gaze lingered on him, especially on his cock, with obvious desire. No fear on this lass's face, despite his size.

At her gesture, he lifted his right leg into the bathing tub—and then cursed at the water's sharp chill. "By Tyr's hand, woman! What mad torture is this?" His voice boomed off the pristine walls, even as he clambered into the cold, fragrant pool.

Laughter burst out of her, shaking her whole body and grabbing his lusty attention once more. "Toughen up, Maximus, we'll bring your sword back to life." With a saucy grin, she joined him in the tub, shivering. As he lowered himself into the bath with a painful hiss, he was delighted to see the effect of the cold water on his Sigyn, his beautiful swan, nipples beaded, her body tightened from the chill.

"Come here, lass," he murmured. "Let my body warm yours."

She drifted closer to him until she sat astride his lap. "Maximus," she whispered, her mouth trailing up his neck toward his beard. Her lips took his in a slow, sensual kiss that restored the heat to his veins. Her softness to his hardness. Her breasts brushing against his thickly furred chest. Her tongue dueling with his. Her teeth taking small, sharp bites from his lower lip before she licked it to soothe the small pinch of pain. Their mouths loved each other for long moments. Bjorn completely forgot himself, where he was, who she was, who he was himself.

There was only this. This woman. This pleasure.

When she sat back with a sultry smile, the soft lips of her sex grazed his erection and he groaned incoherently. To his surprise, she arched back, her abdominal muscles flexing as she dipped her head backwards into the water, now warmed from their bodies. Sweet Asgard, this woman was limber. He ran his fingers over her arching torso, from the indent of her waist to her upthrust breasts that seemed to beg for his touch. He rolled those sweetly pink nipples between the thumb and index finger of both hands, enjoying the sound of her sensual cry at the contact.

But when he leaned forward to take them into his mouth, she pushed him back and gestured to a shallow trough along the side of the tub that contained several small cakes of soap. Realizing she wanted him to lather her hair, he foamed one of the cakes between his palms and then delved his hands into that glorious mane. Her eyes closed in pleasure as he massaged her scalp and drew his fingers down the long length of her tresses, pulling slightly. She leaned back again to rinse the lather from her hair and, when she raised up again, the sunlight glinted off the bright-red strands.

It took him a few moments to notice that her hand was out, silently requesting the soap in his slack fist. When he handed it to her, she rubbed it between her hands slowly and firmly, obviously thinking of something else she could be rolling between those slightly calloused palms.

He dragged in a shaking breath just before she slid her hands into his hair, working the soap in, kneading his skull from the top of his forehead to the base of his neck. He could hear his own groans vibrating off the dazzling white walls of the bathing chamber. Then she paused, looked him square in the eyes and, with a slight smirk, pulled him forward until she'd submerged his head into the water with a splash. Her hands gentled on the back of his head, as he moaned senselessly into the scented water. His nose grazed the inner curve of her breast and, curving his spine, he dragged it lower, tracing the center line of her body to her navel before her hands tightened in his hair, and she jerked him out of the water. His face dripping, he grinned at her, lunged, and wrapped his hands around her slippery form, delighted by her yelp of surprise.

Water sloshed from the tub as they sparred, each grappling with the other only to have their fingers slide away in the slippery, soapy liquid. With a grunt of frustration, Bjorn simply braced his feet and rose from the bath. He looked down upon her, his gorgeous sea goddess, delighted by the way his lover's eyes followed the water sluicing over his muscled body. He stepped out of the tub and then lifted his hand for hers. Pleased that she clasped it firmly, using it for balance as she stepped out to join him, he reached one long arm to pluck a thin towel from a stack. They dried each other with vigorous strokes, and he took a moment to squeeze the water from her hair with the thin, tightly woven linen.

All of the teasing had brought Bjorn to a breaking point. Soon the towel hit the floor, and he was lapping the remaining drops from her shoulders, the dip of her collarbone, the tip of her nipple.

He went to his knees on the soft carpet. Setting his thick hands carefully on her nipped-in waist, he gazed up at her with reverence, asking for permission to continue. When a small smile lifted the corner of her mouth, he licked his tongue against the soft, round flesh of her belly. Keeping his eyes on hers, he trailed the muscle down to the triangle of fiery curls that guarded her sex. Her scent, a mix of the soap's perfume and her own desire, flooded his senses, and he pressed his nose to her hip, inhaling deeply before dragging his nose to her curls.

She gasped when his tongue flicked at the hard nub within her sex. "I see …," her voice had deepened with desire, "that you've found the bud of my rose."

He chuckled into her thigh at her reference to the bawdy tune they'd sung and, to reward her wit, slid the sharp crest of his nose along one side of her rosebud, then the other, then again, until all laughter was gone, and she was moaning rhythmically above him, fingernails digging into his bare, wet shoulders.

Drawing a hand from her waist to her thighs, he teased her nether lips and then the opening of her sex with one blunt finger, slid it into the thick, warm wetness within, licking out his tongue to caress her bud at the same time.

By the gods, she was ready for him.

With one hand on her waist, the other gently pulling outward on her thigh, he urged her downward to where he knelt on the floor of the bathing chamber.

She followed. Her hands on his shoulders, she arranged herself over him, legs astride his kneeling form, lowering herself slowly, slowly, until the wet lips of her sex met the hard tip of his engorged staff. Rubbing her flesh over his, pleasuring herself, her heavy-lidded eyes met his. With a tilt of her hips, she angled herself over his cock and impaled herself in one bold movement that left him gasping for air, barely holding on lest he disgrace himself by coming too soon.

He panted into the column of that long, graceful neck; the pads of his fingers were tight against her hips, holding her still for one excruciating moment, then another. When he brought his head back, he met her eye to eye. With the smallest of movements, they began rocking gently together. His cock deeply buried within her, he ground the bone of his pelvis into her rosebud until her eyes closed and her lips parted. Gradually, he lengthened his thrusts, pulling farther out, then pushing in again, as she moved herself in erotic counterpoint.

"Max …," she whispered, the sound of the name she'd given him trailing off.

But that was not his name.

When he sensed the pleasure rising to its peak within her, he whispered fiercely, "I am Bjorn of Aarhus. *Look at me!*" He needed her to see him, to know him as her lover. He no longer wanted his mask.

Her eyes sprang open, brilliant green, blazing in the shaft of sunlight that warmed their moist bodies. And then he saw her pleasure crest. Her head flung backward, she emitted a throaty shout toward the ceiling, her body clenching tightly, rhythmically against his own. Wrenching his cock from her depths after one last thrust, he pressed it against her belly and came against her, bellowing his pleasure into the damp strands of her sweet-smelling hair.

He clasped her to him, flesh against flesh, as their

bodies rose and fell in their pleasure's aftermath.

To his mind, she was now his bride in truth.

Chapter 4

Much later, as the sun began its descent toward the horizon, Sister Mary Irmengard awoke in her bed with sudden alertness.

Listen first. Then eyes open. Surveil surroundings. Assess threats. If needed, take action.

She knew the drill and practiced it regularly as a discipline, even in the long years of peace at the convent.

Irma realized one thing instantly. She was not alone, her naked body pressed tightly to a man's similarly bare form, a large one at that. Her cheek rested on his chest, tickled slightly by a thick carpet of hair over his well-developed pectoral muscles. Each deep inhale lifted his chest, and then her head. His subsequent exhale blew warm air across her crown, ruffling the unbound strands of her hair. She couldn't deny it was pleasant.

When his next inhale was a rumbling snore, she squelched a flare of amusement. This was no time to underestimate what had occurred.

The Abbey walls had been breached, and she had been seduced out of performing her duty as the guardian general. A creeping shame stole through her. She cringed against the barbarian's hard warmth. She had thought she had suppressed those irrational passions that had authored the most humiliating moments of her life. But as she had survived that betrayal, she would survive this one. No time for self-recriminations.

Assess threats. If needed, take action.

Opening her eyes, she stared out her second floor window and saw that morning had become afternoon. When her stomach gave a little grumble of protest, she realized she'd missed the midday meal, but she willed herself to forget that fact for the moment. Now, she needed to extricate herself from the most serious threat she had encountered since her arrival on the island some fifteen years before. This Maximus had crept through her personal defenses, though she still wasn't sure how.

And he wasn't Maximus, she recalled hazily. In that last moment, a pleasure sharper than she had ever known had gripped her. A pleasure whose mere memory was enough to make her core clench reflexively, forcing her even now to suppress a moan as liquid warmth trickled through her, softening her once more. In that last moment, she recalled, forcing her mind to focus again, in that last moment he had said his name to her.

Bjorn. He was Bjorn of Aarhus.

The name tickled a memory at the back of her brain. Bjorn. Bjorn of Aarhus. Like a dream at the edge of morning, the thought slipped away from her. Even so, she could not shake the idea that she knew this man.

And that he knew her.

From before.

Somehow, he had seduced her into allowing him not only into the Abbey but into her body. Yet Irma was not one to delude herself. As memories of the day flashed through her—the face-off in the courtyard, the wrestling match in the mud that had turned into a sensual battle, their lovemaking (there was no other word for it) in the bathing chamber—Irma knew that she had also seduced him. She was no victim, but a willing partner, in their coupling.

No time for self-recriminations, she reminded herself. Time to take action.

His softly rumbling snores—she finally allowed herself a wry amusement at the sound—assured her that he was unlikely to wake. Nevertheless, she was careful about how she extricated herself from his embrace, easing out from under his arm and backing off her narrow bed until her bare feet touched the cool floor. When he uttered one snuffling murmur before rolling face first into the spot she'd vacated, she held her breath, releasing it only when he fell into gentle snores once more.

She took a minute to observe his features. He had a mass of shaggy brown hair, mostly straight, that covered his neck to its base when he was standing upright. His brow was wide and well-formed, his deep-set eyes heavily lashed, his nose a sharp blade, his cheeks sun-kissed and slightly ruddy above a neatly trimmed beard. *Well-groomed for a barbarian.*

His lips—she faltered a bit at the thought of them—they were a soft pinkish color, his lower lip plumper than the upper. It begged for a kiss, or a bite, and she remembered well the ones she had taken from it, the feel of the warm wet flesh framed by his beard. She shivered slightly and blamed the cool breeze wafting through the narrow window.

Returning to her perusal, she took in his smoothly muscled shoulders, noted with some feminine satisfaction the half-moon marks of her own fingernails embedded in his tanned flesh. Her eyes trailed down his massive chest and thick torso, his hair angling into a line that led to where the thin sheet covered his lean hips.

Bjorn was a bear of a man, indeed, as his name promised.

Despite the immense strength of his form, the way he curled into the bedding and those soft snores suggested a strange kind of vulnerability. It pulled from her an aching tenderness she could not remember having felt ever before.

Irma shook herself. She did not know this man, whatever they had done, whatever familiarity he called forth from within her. Whatever he looked like curled into her bed linens.

No matter any of that, she could not trust him.

What were these men doing here? What was their aim? It was her duty to find out and to return the Abbey to its previous, peaceful, man-free state.

Quashing the slight pang at the thought, she became suddenly alert to her own nudity.

With the thought that these men who had invaded the convent would not be expelled through traditional battle, Irma dug from a low bureau her more typical attire of a high-necked, cream-colored tunic belted over leather trousers. As she dressed, she inventoried the effects of Maximus's—or rather, Bjorn's—attentions, small, pinkening marks made by erotic scratches, sucking lips, the scrape of his beard on her tender flesh. When she caught herself tracing one love bite at the top of her breast, she scolded herself and deliberately covered the evidence of their mating with the modest garment.

Belting her tunic, she fingered the thick strip of material shrewdly. It might be wise to bind her captive while he slept. Perhaps she could interrogate him. With a glance at his still slumbering form, she discarded the idea. She was slightly disgusted with herself to admit that, if he woke as she tied him, she'd likely end up back in bed with him.

It was good to know one's own weaknesses.

She needed distance from him to regain her wits. To develop a clear strategy.

This wasn't running away. It was a strategic retreat.

Aware that, even in retreat, one must be armed, she tucked an array of small but sharp weapons into their various sheaths on her belt. Efficiently pulling her wildly curling hair into a hasty braid that curved over her collarbone, Irma eased out of her room and into the convent hallway. She pulled the door softly closed behind her and left her captor to his sleep—well-earned as it was, she acknowledged with a wry twist of her lips.

Out in the corridor, it was eerily quiet. So quiet, she heard the lazy buzzing of a bee as it drifted out one of the long narrow windows near the stairs.

Those hazy memories of hers reminded her that, when she and Bjorn had ascended the stairway, the hall had been full of sound. There were signs that other sisters had also found themselves engaged with the barbarians—and wasn't that a peculiar thought, Irma realized. She was not the only one who had broken form. Shaking her head with exasperation, she stepped over a heap of cloth that appeared to be a hastily discarded wimple, then a man's large leather boot.

For an instant, she wondered whether the men had cast some enchanted spell over them all. But then, with a deep knowing in her gut, she understood that this was the island's magic at work.

She reckoned the sensual fog had not cleared from her brain, and so the enchantment must still linger. First, she would assess the damage. Then she would find the key to end the enchantment and expel the male invaders, forever. To do that, she would need the assistance of at least one of the other nuns. Surely, someone had proven resistant to the sybaritic magic that had engulfed their dwelling.

Together, they would restore their peace, she vowed, forcing her resolve to drown out a whisper of longing for a different future.

No, they must not forget what they had come from. She must not forget what she had survived—and what she had no desire to live through again.

****

Bjorn of Aarhus was dreaming.

In the dream, women wailed. His hands, though he did not see them, dripped with blood, rendering them too slick to be useful. One woman, the one he could not tear his eyes from, was utterly silent. Her hair lay in damp strands around her forehead, her mouth parted, inaudibly panting. Her eyes, though, her eyes pleaded with him, begged him to help her.

Accused him.

You did this.

He could not look away.

He could hear the indictment even through her silence, past the howls of grief around him. It pounded in the rapid thump of his heartbeat. Guilt.

In the dream, he roared out his own pain, and the world shook around him.

He awoke on a soundless gasp.

It took him several moments to steady himself, which he did with some effort. He concentrated on scanning and cataloguing his surroundings. Bare white walls. Bright light through a skinny window. Low wooden bureau, finely crafted. Narrow bed draped in a white sheet. A quiet hum of activity from somewhere nearby.

He was alone.

No blood.

The sorrows were old, the wounds covered over with scars.

He hadn't had the dream in a very long time, but part of him wasn't surprised it had returned. And returned when it had.

Bjorn knew where he was, had known it instantly, and he recalled in vivid detail every moment that had passed since he and the other men had landed on this island in the mist. He recalled every minute of his erotic dance with the person who had haunted his deepest fantasies for the last decade and a half. A woman of strength, loyalty, courage. But a woman all the same.

A woman who had left him here alone.

Drawing his hand over his damp face, the wet a combination of sweat and tears, he pulled in a stuttering breath and shook off the dream. The past was past.

After the tragedy, he had made a vow, and he had kept it through the years without much effort. Until today. His vow lay broken, but he found he could not be sorry for it.

Casting a glance around the room, he supposed he should be grateful that his lover had not tied him to the bed—or killed him in his sleep, he thought ruefully. Still, it stung that she had left him after what they had shared. Now that she knew his name.

He wasn't sure she knew *him* yet. But she would.

Because he was determined to have her.

Though wise enough to understand that she would have the final say, he was yet man enough to feel confident that he could persuade her. What they had between them was a miracle, and he would grab onto it, by Freya's feathered cloak. The first arrows of battle had been fired, true, but there was a longer war to be waged. Bjorn was not a man to give up.

No matter the dream and its accusations. No matter his guilt. No matter the blood on his hands.

This warrior woman would be his. He would not do to her what he had done to his wife. That was a vow he would keep.

His fingers toyed with the hair over his top lip. To win her, he would need to lay a careful strategy.

All the more careful since he knew she'd be doing the same.

Chapter 5

Sister Mary Irmengard did not yet have a strategy. Though she was pleased to don once more her cool, clear-headed mantle as chief guardian of Adytum, she recognized that she confronted her most serious challenge yet. Dispelling the sensual spell that engulfed them and expelling the barbarians would be no simple task. How many were there? How deeply had they penetrated the convent walls? What had brought them to the island? Would they loot and pillage and then leave?

Or might they seek to remain?

Irma was astute enough to know what she did not yet know. Shrewd enough to seek out information from others at the Abbey.

And so, like any good general, she spent her next hours taking stock, surveying the field of battle the convent had become. The gnawing in her gut had demanded, out of practicality, that her first stop be the dining hall. The Abbey's cook, Sister Benita, she was surprised to see, had been cheerfully serving up steaming meat pies and ale to both women and men seated in small groupings along the wooden banquet tables. Though Benita was almost always good-humored—especially when feeding people—Irma was confounded at her unbothered response to the presence of men, barbarians at that, at their tables, who demanded food outside of the conventional mealtimes.

"Everyone has to eat," she'd said pragmatically when Irma asked her about it around her own mouthful of the fragrant pastry. Then Benita had bustled off to the kitchen for more trays of food, appearing happy as a clam at high water.

The cook seemed the only one of the sisters not attached to a man, Irma had realized, noting the intimacy of the pairs and clusters of men and women around the dining hall. Hands laid over hands, noses buried in necks, mouths whispering in ears. Two of the sisters sat on their barbarians' laps, apparently without a care. But her gaze caught on one man, clean-shaven with a mop of black hair, who sat by himself and whose eyes followed Sister Benita where she disappeared into the kitchen. The hunger in his expression was plainly not for food.

Irma had taken it all in and calculated: enchantment. The island had bewitched all of them. There was no other conceivable answer. Soon, as she herself had experienced, her sisters would wake up. And then what? And what of the men when the magic spell faded?

Determinedly not thinking of the man she'd left in her own bed, who might even now find his attachment to her fading, Irma finished her meal quickly and exited through a back door that led to an outside quadrangle of buildings. Time to survey the field of battle.

The convent's main building now lay behind her. Benita's kitchens were situated in a smaller, one-story building in front of her, while the dairy barn and small work shed formed the sides of the small square.

This is strange. She paced the yard looking for signs of distress, clues to the men's purpose on the island. Despite the earlier chaos, all now seemed …normal, quiet even. She suppressed her frustration, reminding herself she was cool and rational once more. No need to rush her patrol of the island.

Reckoning that if there were immediate threats here, Benita had her chance to mention them, Irma went back into the dining hall and into the convent's large foyer. The door to the Music Chamber had been forcibly opened, likely kicked in. She imagined how it must have happened as she walked across the stone floor of the main hall in long strides. Pulling a dagger from her belt, she stepped into the room but saw immediately that it had been abandoned and left in total disarray. Scanning for lingering threats and seeing none, she tucked away her weapon and bent to examine the wreckage of their Music Chamber. They were only days away from the spring ritual that featured the island's musical celebrations of new life. Irma spied the opening in the stone floor where the convent musician Sister Frances had been stashing the precious instruments before obviously being interrupted.

Poor Sister Frances. Concern filled her at the thought. Smallish, artistic, and sensitive, she'd have been no match for these brutes. When a scrap of white caught her eye, she lifted it, recognizing it as a wimple from a nun's habit that had been discarded on the stone floor. Over there was a pair of shoes that had been kicked off and lay untidily in a corner of the room.

Perhaps, Irma considered with a twist of her mouth, her concern was misplaced. *Enchantment.* She shook her head in exasperation.

Nothing more to be learned from the Music Chamber, Irma headed through the foyer toward the convent's entrance. With the feeling of returning to the scene of a terrible accident, Irma stepped out through the wide double doors that had protected the Abbey from all previous threats. Those doors now stood open, the wooden planks splintered. Not that she wouldn't have willingly opened them herself, given the state she'd been in when she'd been carried—carried!—across the threshold only hours ago. She huffed in self-disgust.

Irma forced her attention back to the present. Though the barbarians had won the initial battle, she and her sisters could turn the tide if they had the right information. They had to know their enemy.

With that in mind, Irma scanned the inner courtyard. That last battlefield stood empty. Determinedly, she ignored the muddy patch several yards in front of the door where she and her barbarian had …tangled. Such a memory was, at present, irrelevant.

The glint of a blade caught her eye, and when she turned her head, she spied her sword. With a small cry, she rushed over to the bramble bush that held it. Cursing, she disentangled it from the brambles' sharp clutches. Once it was released, she breathed a sigh of relief to find it undamaged and slid it into the sheath on her belt. She gave her hips a little swivel. That was better. Balanced.

Casting her view across the courtyard, she could see the deep footprints in the mud where the men, having climbed the eight-foot stone walls that circled the wide space, had jumped down into the inner sanctum.

They should never have gotten that far.

Following their tracks through the courtyard gate and toward the shore, many yards away and through a dense path of brambles, Irma found three longboats along the water's edge, hastily abandoned. Though too small to be a typical raiding party, their presence indicated far too many men in their women-only refuge.

In all likelihood, Irma realized, she and her sisters were outnumbered.

She paused at the shoreline, inhaling the salty ocean breeze, allowing the gentle lapping of waves to settle her.

The boats were well-made, she observed, gliding her hand up the keel to the curving stempost at the front of the ship. These were quite secure vessels, with a hull that would keep out water, and sported fine cloth sails. “Perhaps not of the highest quality,” she mused, playing her fingers along the boat’s rather plain exterior. Though the stempost of each swept up into a fine scroll, it was nonetheless a rather simpler design than the dragons or gorgons featured on the showiest crafts. Free of the elaborate carvings of royal ships she’d once seen, these boats were more like the ones she’d served on and likely belonged to the wealthy chief of a smaller territory. Thus, she deduced with some relief, this was probably not the expedition of a great king. Though there was wealth and power here, to be sure, perhaps not so much that they could expect reinforcements to arrive. That was at least some comfort.

Clambering aboard, Irma maneuvered through the abandoned oars and other detritus left on board when the vessels had made land. Alas, a thorough search of the ships’ interiors turned up nothing that provided a clue as to their purpose here. Irma found stores of salted fish and hard flour biscuits—thank the goddess she no longer subsisted on that. A shudder rippled through her at the memory. The men had packed a standard change of clothing, so perhaps the journey had been long, or they anticipated a lengthy stay. Irma firmed her jaw. Not if she had anything to say about it.

Noting that a surprising number of shields had been

left behind amid the rowing benches, Irma flushed with ire that the barbarians had judged their victory so easy. She tried to let the violent emotion drain from her, expelling it on a deep exhale.

"Well, maybe you have had an easy time of it to this point." She shot an irritated look at the Abbey whose fortified doors stood wide open. "But you men may well need your shields before all is said and done," she muttered to the scattered objects around her. She returned to her careful search of what she concluded to be fairly ordinary pillaging ships.

The last boat, however—it held an unexpected treasure. Digging under one of the long benches, Irma discovered an oiled cloth wrapped around some hard, loose objects. *Probably loot from some poor village*. But when she unwrapped it, she hooted in delight. Instead of the jewels she'd expected, she held in her hands a mix of black and white game pieces, skillfully carved out of bone. So skillfully, indeed, that she could make out comical features on the faces of pawns, more sophisticated expressions on the knights, queens, and kings, one with nostrils flaring in anger, the other with somber, slanting brows.

Chess! She hadn't played since—her mind skittered over the memory. It had been a long time, but she had enjoyed the game of war and strategy. A little more digging revealed a folded game board woven from flax into alternating dark and light squares. Evidently well used, it was somewhat frayed in places but nevertheless serviceable. With no small measure of satisfaction, Irma wrapped her booty securely in its cloth and tucked it snugly in the long pocket of her tunic so that her hands remained free.

Leaving everything else behind, especially the cured herring, Irma descended from the last boat and made her way from the sandy shore toward the Abbey.

Once back behind the high courtyard walls, Irma looked out toward the rhythmically churning waves of the sea. *We'll send you back the way you came*, she vowed, thinking of the men and pleased to know she'd keep their game behind with her.

As a reminder.

Because someday this would all be just a memory.

On an impulse whose origin she could not identify, Irma paused at one of the long, waist-high tables that lay in shadow in the main hall's entry. Unwrapping her stolen loot, she carefully set up the artfully carved game pieces on their woven field of battle. When she'd placed the final piece, she stood back to admire the stage she had built. Whimsically, she took a frightened-looking white pawn and moved it forward one space.

Battle engaged.

Though it may take many moves, she would corner the barbarians' king, she pledged, whoever he was, and knock every last man off her island.

Checkmate.

If Irma didn't recognize the bear-like face of the white knight, that was her mistake.

****

"For the love of Baldr, that is a good pie," Bjorn declared around a hot mouthful of pastry. He was feeling rather more cheerful after some restorative food and drink.

Less than an hour ago, he'd roused himself in search of his lover …and food. He was a man of lusty appetites. Food and drink were objects of physical desire he'd freely indulged in these last years, while he'd declined to pursue others.

Somewhat surprised to find his clothing clean and folded in one of his lover's dresser-drawers, he felt not-at-all apologetic about investigating the bureau's intimate contents. He needed to know his adversary in this erotic game they waged together. Perhaps she'd expected no better of him, since his clothes were neatly tucked inside, as if waiting for him. But he rather thought that, somehow, someone other than she was the responsible party.

Bjorn had dressed and peeked curiously into a now-spotless bathing chamber. Ostensibly on the hunt for his woman, he'd been lured downstairs by the delicious scent of roasted meat.

Which he now thoroughly enjoyed. His recent activities had certainly depleted his energies. By Odin's beard, he'd been famished.

"Why, thank you," said a mellifluous voice above him, having heard his comment about the hand pie.

A rosy-cheeked maid cloaked in white stood beside where he sat at the long bench of the dining table. She clasped a stack of wooden platters in her hand, replicas of the one that still held half of his pie.

"And did you make it then?"

Hearing skepticism in his voice, the plump-cheeked nun's expression tightened. "That I did." Her voice had cooled considerably. "Does that alter your assessment of it?"

Bjorn set down his flagon to raise both hands. "No, indeed, fair sister, and I ask your pardon. It's the best pie I can remember having anywhere." When she continued to stare at him, apparently unimpressed by his bland though completely accurate compliment, he added, "The crust is flaky but strong enough to hold." An encouraging look had him reaching further. He picked up the pie, took another bite. "The meat is tender, well-seasoned with a combination of herbs that warms the senses. It is—" he chewed thoughtfully and hoped he was not laying it all on rather too thickly, "—a masterpiece."

After a short pause, the nun smiled at him. "Then you are welcome." She gave him a gracious nod, her voice warm again.

It occurred to him that she might be a good source of information about his absent bride and the island on which he'd found her. Thus, when the chef nun made to leave, he stopped her with a question he thought might ingratiate him enough to prolong the conversation. "I'm surprised you haven't used fish. Where do you get the meat?"

Lips pursed, she said, "From the sheep, of course."

So this was not a maid to be flattered into a revealing conversation, more's the pity. The information that there were sheep on the island was …not at all useful.

This time, when she made to leave, he dared to place a hand briefly on her arm, lifting it high again when her gaze turned sharp. Nothing for it but a direct question. "One of your number, a warrior with"—he wisely refrained from outlining the shape of her glorious bosom and curved-in waist, gesturing instead to his head—"bright-red hair. Very"—*sensual*—"strong and"—*passionate enough to bring a man to his knees*—"martial," he concluded.

The sister's gaze grew speculative. "What of her?"

What of her? The defensive question struck him hard. What did he want to know? That which moved her.

Brought her joy. Made her laugh. That which would soften her toward him. Bjorn wanted the key to winning her heart and proving his worth to her. Was that too much to ask?

Right at this moment, though, he wanted to know, where was she?

Realizing this sister was not the fount of information he'd hoped, he settled for asking a question to which he thought he might receive an answer. "Her name?" He tried for a guileless expression.

The sister stalked off with a huff but then hesitated and returned. "Sister Mary Irmengard," she said abruptly. "Irma." Looking slightly angry at herself, the nun spun quickly on her heel and marched toward a door at the back of the dining hall.

Bjorn did not watch her go. The name, her name, drew his entire focus.

Mary, drop of the sea. Irmengard, the strong protector.

He'd known her by another name, of course. And then yet another. All fit her, in their own way. But this name she bore now, he could see how well it suited her.

Never one to let good food go to waste, Bjorn returned his attention to the very fine pie and his mug of ale. A man had to fuel his energies when he had a battle to wage.

Licking his fingers a short while later and taking a long look at the white walls around him, Bjorn mused that, just perhaps, the talented cook had given him the key to victory after all.

Chapter 6

More than Fifteen Years Ago

"Ah, you've beaten me again!" young Signus grumbled, after taking a long look at the board. He tossed a pawn in the direction of the checkered cloth that was their playing field.

Bjorn caught the piece swiftly. "You're just learning, whelp. You want me to beat you. What kind of teacher would I be if I couldn't beat someone who's only played a handful of games? Always play someone better than you."

"You've played a lot then?"

"Of course! What else is there to do in the long wintertime?"

A few men who'd observed the game offered some bawdy suggestions, and the two players grinned at one another.

"Aye, very well, but a man needs rest, you know," Bjorn called over his shoulder.

"Chess is so complicated," Signus complained. "What about Nine Men's Morris?" Signus could beat anyone at that game.

Bjorn scoffed. "Nine Men's Morris is for children."

"Hey, I like Nine Men's Morris!" called out one of the other men, one Signus had beaten on quite a few occasions.

"Once you've learned the secret to winning, there's no contest in it," Bjorn said dismissively. "Chess, on the other hand, has many, many paths to victory—and defeat. It sharpens the senses." He tapped his temple. "Develops the mind. It's as important as knowing how to wield your sword." He wasn't second-in-command of the band for nothing. This was an important part of any lad's training but, both men knew, especially needed in this beardless one's instruction, as he was smaller, younger, and more inexperienced than most of the others.

Several rude remarks followed at this pompousness, but Bjorn ignored them. He was setting up the pieces again. White for Signus—they'd joked that his name meant "the swan," after all—and black for Bjorn. He didn't mind. As he told Signus, he rather liked the expression on the black king's face.

Signus visibly shook off his disappointment and began reconfiguring the board on his side. Without looking up, he said, "Do you think I could ever be as good at this as you?"

Bjorn paused for a long moment. So long that Signus raised bright green eyes to meet his teacher's hazel ones.

When Bjorn had Signus's full attention, he spoke to him in a low voice so the others would not hear. "You have a brain, Signus." His words were not so much a compliment as an observation. "A good one. Someday, you'll have a band of your own if you take the time to learn tactics and strategy and not just methods of brute strength, like most of those." He tipped his head to the men. "Brute strength isn't *your* strength anyway," he added. "No, that was not an insult, Signus," he said, at the young man's ruffling feathers. "It's no more than the truth. You know it yourself. Physical force can only do so much. I've seen you fight in such a way that uses your opponent's own force against him or that uses unpredictability to win the fight. You're also a very competent negotiator already, and this your first spring plundering season. You're a fine soldier. As good a man as we've got, for all that you are young."

Signus's eyes lowered, seeming uncomfortable with the praise. *As good a man as we've got.* Bjorn's compliment hung in the air.

"You just need experience. And," Bjorn said with a grin, "to keep playing chess with me."

Breaking the seriousness of the moment, he added, "Someday you'll be a worthy opponent," and caught this time the white queen when Signus threw it at him.

His boisterous laugh merged with Signus's, and the two warriors settled in for another match.

****

The Present

Her most important business, Irma knew, was identifying the king she had to topple—that is, the barbarians' leader who had brought them here. Even if she didn't find him immediately, she could learn his purpose here, and that would prove useful in ejecting him and his confounded band of confederates.

Ideally, she would capture one of the barbarians and get the information from him. She was no torturer but had found that bargaining with barbarians—who, she thought derisively, generally had quite low levels of honor and loyalty—often enough did the trick. One just needed to know what to trade for. As the island had always provided, she was confident that she could arrange a barter for information without too much trouble. In the event of reluctance, a sharp knife at the neck would also incline them toward dealmaking. She just needed to find one of the men and, with a combination of duress and negotiation, she'd have the facts she needed.

But finding one of the men on his own, without a sister quite literally attached, proved more challenging than she had expected.

Knowing now that the men outnumbered the women, she'd thought surely there would be men roaming about on their own. Yet everywhere she looked, the men—sometimes singly but sometimes in pairs and even more—had bonded with her sisters. An intimate-bond decency made her reluctant to interrupt.

Even the lone man in the dining hall, the one sitting by himself mooning after Sister Benita, had evidently moved along, though she knew not where. Perhaps Benita was no longer alone, either.

Alert to potential threats, Irma had peeked her head in the Worship Chamber, a vast, high-ceilinged room lined with stained glass that cast gaily colored beams of light about the floor and walls. She pulled her head back quickly when she realized a couple was erotically engaged on the altar itself, their limbs entwined, bodies joined and moving sensually together. For a moment, she wondered whether she saw a couple …or more? Another quick peek confirmed the latter and reminded her to keep her curiosity to herself.

But on the altar! For the love of the goddess, had they no respect?

She was chastened by a flash of memory of her rolling in the mud with her bear—not *her bear*, she reminded herself grimly, but Bjorn. She was in no position to judge. And the goddess did not seem displeased, after all.

That thought brought Irma up short like a hard slap.

Was the goddess in league with these barbarian invaders? It seemed impossible, given all of Irma's experience with the loving, divine force of the island. But how else to explain the ease with which these men had breached walls that had stood strong for as long as Irma had lived here—and even before? She remembered the feeling she'd had during the courtyard battle, the feeling that the goddess had extended her protection to the men.

Could it be so? What would that mean?

Interpreting the will of the goddess was not her particular gift, but there were others who might have glimpsed the purpose in all of this.

So Irma had moved along to the side chambers of the vast ritual space, empty but containing evidence of libidinous interactions in a scattering of both male and female clothing. Then she'd climbed up a spiraling stone staircase to the Abbey's Library, where she finally found some sisters who seemed free of the sexual haze that engulfed the rest of the Abbey's residents. Sisters of strong mind and divinely inspired insight. Sisters who had mastered the wisdom of the Abbey's most precious documents, gathered over years and decades, if not centuries.

The Library was a room of both bright sunlight and dense shadows. A dark portion of the chamber was given over to rows and rows of books and scrolls, tidily organized away from the damaging rays of the sun. If they hadn't known before, the women who came to the island were sooner or later taught to read the basic scripts that conveyed the goddess's benevolence and the sisters' ritual acknowledgement of it through the seasons. They undertook these lessons in the brightly lit eastern corner of the chamber which caught the morning sun in two large windows.

Yet most of the texts could not be easily deciphered regardless, written in multiple languages of which the island's women had no prior knowledge. The books' Keeper, and her assistant, carried the charge of learning and interpreting the ancient sources for the convent. Although most of the documents were freely available to anyone, other texts were hidden away more deeply, their location a closely guarded secret only the Keeper knew.

At the room's center, part in light and part in shadow, stood a large table that was most frequently empty. At present, Irma noted, on its surface lay a variety of books and scrolls, some opened, some closed, all strewn haphazardly in a manner that suggested haste—or even panic.

In this chamber, Irma had fully expected to find Sister Alice, Keeper of the Sacred Scripts. The Library was her domain after all. Though reserved and intellectual, Sister Alice held the quiet authority that came from knowing the island's secrets. Irma was counting on Alice to know some tricks that might be used against the thugs who had invaded their refuge.

She also anticipated finding here young Sister Grace, Alice's sweet-natured assistant who most often taught basic literacy to the island's new arrivals.

Both women were indeed present. But two other women also gathered around the large center table. The island's sage, Sister Catherine of the Oracle, stood somewhat to the side. Standing in front of the table was the Mother Superior, Sister Agnes of the Holy Water, a tall blonde somewhat older than Irma whose confident command kept the Abbey running smoothly and harmoniously.

Irma had evidently interrupted a tactical meeting—one to which she had not been invited. She suppressed a flare of irritation. This was a time to maintain her professionalism as chief guardian.

At the moment, quite uncharacteristically, they were arguing.

"I'm only telling you what the ancient texts indicate—" the bookish Sister Alice was saying forcefully to the Mother Superior.

"That cannot be the case." The Mother's reply was sharp. "There must be a way—"

Agnes stopped abruptly when Catherine raised her head to look where Irma stood quietly in the doorway, the only one to have sensed her presence in the heat of their argument. The others moved their gazes to where Catherine stared, and Irma found herself the focus of attention.

"Sister Mary Irmengard," Mother Agnes said in calmer tones. Irma noticed that she moved her body to block Irma's view of a large tome open behind her on the Library table. "How fare you?"

Irma sensed the Mother's careful perusal of her features. *Undoubtedly looking for signs of uncontrolled lust*. Well, she had shaken that off—never mind the small pang at the thought of how she'd left Bjorn in her bed. She had information to share. If they were to eject the barbarians, they would need to work together even more tightly than usual.

"I have …recovered." She figured it was better to be honest. For all she knew, these women had similarly woken up from sexual enchantments of their own. In fact, both the Mother Superior and the Oracle had their heads bared instead of covered as they usually did. Irma's keen eyes scanned the room's occupants and found other small signs of disorder. One of Sister Alice's sleeves appeared tucked under itself, as if quickly donned. And although Sister Grace's hair was covered, Irma spied a love mark just below her jawline. So. She was indeed not alone. Nevertheless, as the front line of defense, she had borne the most responsibility to resist.

Bowing her head, she let genuine remorse color her reply. "I apologize most deeply for my lapse that allowed the barbarians entrance to the Abbey."

The Mother waved a dismissive hand, still examining Irma's features. "Do not concern yourself overly, Sister Mary Irmengard. It appears to have been *inevitable*." Her lip twisted at the corner. The willowy woman cast an irritated glance at Sister Catherine who merely shrugged in response. "And it appears that most of our sisters have …succumbed …in one way or another to the barbarians' …charms." A strange expression passed across her visage. "Now we must see about sending them on their way again."

"I am in perfect agreement," Irma said quickly.

"Well, then, we must confer. Please join us." Agnes backed away from the table to make room for Irma.

"Though Sister Catherine did have some inkling of these events"—another pointed glare at the Oracle—"she did not learn of it in time. Nor did she see any way to avoid the …effects."

"It does appear," Irma interjected, "that the island's

spirit is not opposed to these men's incursions. The barbarians navigated to the island, which we know is not easily discovered. They managed the bramble path from the shore and scaled the courtyard walls without much difficulty. Once the men were within the walls, our weapons drew no blood. However, we should note that theirs also drew no blood. And I believe them to be similarly"—she struggled with the word for a moment, before settling on—"*bespelled.* They did not act like any warriors that I have seen." A memory flashed through her of Bjorn bowing to her, sword down, eyes filled with masculine mischief.

Mother Agnes's expression softened in relief. "I am glad to hear that we at least have no blood spilled on our side. However, there appear to be several of our sisters missing. I can't even begin to know how to account for everyone."

"Aye, I inspected the men's vessels, and given the number and size of their ships, the barbarians most likely outnumber us. Their patron is no doubt wealthy, but not of the highest royalty. I regret that I was not able to discern their purpose in coming here."

The four women exchanged glances. "As to that, Sister Mary Irmengard, I believe we now hold that answer." Mother Agnes straightened with determination. "Their leader's name is Harald. Sister Frances, who encountered him, described him as violent and unpredictable. He is here to find Astrid, who lately arrived on our shores."

"Astrid!" Irma herself had brought the young woman into the convent not two weeks before.

Irma had an instinct for sensing new arrivals to the island, a gift from the goddess, she assumed. Most of the time, she discovered women, soon-to-be-sisters, washed up either bodily or with their vessels, and most often on the eastern, sandy side of the island.

"Strangely, I found Astrid on the western side of the island instead of the eastern beach," Irma reminded the other women in the room. "She had foundered on the rocks in a small, hole-riddled craft but had climbed out onto a boulder to get to drier ground before losing consciousness. She was …not in good physical health."

Irma's jaw clenched at the memory of the rag-covered body she had found, limp and dirty but miraculously alive. The pale woman's face and arms were mottled with bruises, her torn fingernails suggesting that she had fought someone to escape. Most likely, that someone was this violent Harald they had mentioned. *Now I know the Black King.*

Fleeing violent men was not an unusual story for the island's refugees, but it evoked Irma's sympathies nonetheless. *Poor woman. We will protect you from your pursuer.*

"Has she regained consciousness?"

"Not as of yet," Sister Grace's sweet, high-pitched voice offered tentatively. Sister Grace was a close friend of Mother Agnes's daughter, who oversaw the ward on which new arrivals recovered and were introduced to the Abbey. Grace put a finger to her temple. "Bad dreams, though."

"This Harald," Irma continued. "If Sister Frances encountered him, he must have been responsible for the damage in the Music Chamber. I did not see him when I patrolled the Abbey, however."

"We have not been able to locate him," Sister Catherine said.

"What does he look like?" Irma asked.

"Unfortunately," Sister Catherine sent a sharp glance to Mother Agnes this time, "we do not have a description of him."

"Sister Frances did not see him?"

"She did indeed encounter him, but she fainted before she could provide us with a full description." Mother Agnes's tone was deliberately neutral.

"Fainted!" Sister Frances was quiet but had a strong will underneath. Irma would not have imagined her fainting except under the most extreme pressure. "Is she in the sick ward now, as well?"

Agnes and Catherine exchanged another cryptic look. "Yes, and it would not do to disturb her," the Mother said. "She needs to rest."

"Besides, she is unlikely to recall encountering this Harald when she revives," Sister Catherine added.

"Why is that?" Irma frowned. Beneath the surface, a debate was going on between the Mother Superior and the Oracle, and Irma was irritated not to be privy to the whole story.

"It is no matter." Mother Agnes waved a dismissive hand. "We shall see when she wakes, but that is unlikely to be for several hours."

"In any case," Sister Catherine chimed in again, "this Harald has not disguised himself and has made his mission clear. He intends to take Astrid away with him. We shall not allow that to happen."

"But Sister Catherine, as I was saying—" interrupted Alice, Keeper of the Sacred Scripts, who had previously watched the interchange silently.

Mother Agnes turned to her. "You must be in error," she said sharply.

A tense silence descended on the room. The harshness of the Mother's tone was uncharacteristic, and Irma found herself wondering what had happened to their usually unflappable leaders.

"Tell me, Sister Alice." Irma pitched her voice to an encouraging murmur.

With some exasperation, Alice pointed toward the large tome in the middle of the pile of scrolls and books on the center table. Irma noticed that the other woman's hand shook and recalled that Alice had encountered such seafaring barbarians previously, in her life before the island. She was likely terrified at the prospect of facing their brutality again. "As you well know, Irma," Alice said, in a nevertheless steady voice, "there is no way to leave the island."

Irma's brow furrowed. "That is for the sisters who come here. We have expelled invaders."

Sister Alice's mouth grew taut. "Only while they were still in the waters around the island. The few times men have set foot on our land," she reminded her audience, "we dispatched them in the only permanent way." The Keeper swallowed audibly.

Irma drew her head back. "We killed them," she said, remembering it with no pleasure. "But they were thieves and murderers."

"As are these!" Mother Agnes pointed out hotly.

"Are they?" The smaller voice of Sister Grace came out as a mere whisper but nevertheless echoed in the room.

A long silence followed as all four women pondered the question.

Irma found herself thinking of Bjorn. A feeling deep within her resisted the idea of him as a knave. No, he was not of the same ilk as the bad actors who had previously gained access to the island. She thought of how he had bowed to her, his argument with Minimus about fighting her, his good-humored parrying of her taunts, his following her lead in their erotic dance.

Perhaps the other sisters felt the same about the men they had engaged with sensually. She could hardly blame them, considering her own mixed feelings about the powerful but surprisingly gentle bear who had seduced her.

We seduced each other. She must remember that salient fact.

He had certainly allowed her to direct their sexual war of wills. Memories assailed her of the way she had pulled his hair to guide him up to her bedchamber. The way she had boldly stripped herself of all arms and clothing, with no fear of such vulnerability. The way she had joined their bodies in the bathing chamber and ridden him to their mutual climax.

Annoyed that her body went liquid at the thought, she shook off the memory.

"Anyway, there were not so many of them before," she said briskly.

On only two previous occasions had men set foot on the island in the fifteen years Irma had been here. One man had come alone, sneaking onto the beach while she'd slept in her chamber. At dawn's break, she had awoken with a start and, with that supernatural knowing of hers, promptly discovered him atop one of the sisters in her bedchamber, having climbed in a window and pressed a knife to the other woman's throat.

Irma had killed him outright and had no remorse for what she saw as a necessary action.

The others had been a pair that had arrived with a woman between them. Nasty pieces of work, those two, and she'd had no doubt about their violent plans for the woman. With the aid of another island guardian, Irma had battled the two to the death, settled their bodies unceremoniously in their small boat, and sent them back into the sea, from whence they'd never returned. Their intended victim had joined the Abbey as a valued sister in the convent.

But such a course of action was not possible with these barbarians and their three longboats. "They outnumber us this time," she reminded the other four women, "and we can hardly kill upwards of seventy men."

"Yes, that is what we were just discussing." Sister Alice gestured again to the pile of books on the table. "I am afraid the sacred texts have little to offer if we hope to repulse the men now that they have made land." Alice spoke with an air of distraction, her finger tracing a line in the large tome before her. Sister Grace made a small noise.

"Yet you see something there? Some alternative?" Irma asked.

"No, she does not," said Mother Agnes repressively. Alice opened her mouth as if to disagree but then shrugged. Grace leaned up to whisper in Alice's ear. Alice responded in a brief, fierce interchange, inaudible to the other women, before turning back to them. Irma narrowed her gaze at them, aware that they were not sharing everything they knew.

"I will keep looking," Alice said doubtfully, "though I do not recall any provisions for calling upon the goddess to send away such a quantity of men as this."

When Agnes looked as if she might speak again, Alice added, "But I will continue to search."

"As I will stay open to the will of the goddess." Sister Catherine of the Oracle ran a frustrated hand over her bare head. "For now, she is quiet, though not sleeping. Her will is …blocked from me."

"Actively blocked?" Irma asked. A benevolent presence, the island's goddess was not usually so mysterious. "Could a priest among the men have conjured interference between you and the goddess?"

"I do not know." A frown appeared between Catherine's dark-winged brows. "Though I had fragments of warning, none were clear enough to act upon, not until the danger was already upon us. And since the men have arrived"—she lifted her hands helplessly—"she is present within me, but …quiet."

Agnes tapped her nail on the book Alice had opened. "The ritual *ceolchoirm* celebrates the coming of spring and worships the goddess. It's to be performed at the spring equinox in two days. Can we use it to direct the island's feminine energy against the men?"

This suggestion provoked another guarded glance between Alice and Grace. Then Alice said, "I shall investigate that possibility. Perhaps with some adjustment the music might become a call for the goddess's assistance in our particular circumstances."

"Once she is feeling better, Sister Frances will be able to help." Mother Agnes injected cheerful optimism into her voice. "She is such a gifted musician. In presiding over the musical part of the ritual, she will be able to reverse the enchantment that brought these men here and that lulls us into accepting their presence."

"If I may?" To Irma's surprise, Grace had piped up,

her hand raised for their attention. The young woman swallowed nervously before continuing. "We should also remember that the *ceolchoirm* ritual is about transformation and the sprouting of new life—"

A sharp look from Alice suddenly silenced her, and Grace snapped her mouth closed.

"We will see what may be possible," said Alice repressively. "However, I wouldn't count on the equinox ritual of *ceolchoirm,* Mother Agnes. Though the texts hint at—" Alice stopped self-consciously. Grace poked her in the ribs, to which Alice responded with a quick shake of her head. "The texts do not, in any case, offer the possibility of expelling these men en masse."

Feeling frustrated, Irma straightened. "If we cannot access the will of the goddess nor use sacred rituals, we will simply have to use cunning and strategy." This was her strength, after all, and she would deploy it to the best of her ability.

Leaving the tableside, she paced the room, first toward the dark corner with the scrolls and then toward the brightly lit reading corner in the east, and back again, and again. The other women watched her and waited.

Finally, Irma drew herself to a halt at the center of the room, aware that all eyes were on her. "My assessment of the men is that they are not an immediate violent danger to us, except"—she raised a finger—"for their leader, this Harald." She looked from one sister to the next, weighing her next actions. "First, I will send guardians to protect Astrid in the sick ward. She is the one most in danger, and we must guard her well."

"Be sure that their presence does not signal to anyone that Harald's prize lies within," Mother Agnes said.

Irma nodded. "Of course. Our priority should be to intercept Harald. Though I have no description of him, he should be easy enough to discover as he does not seem to care to hide his identity or the target of his quest. Once we have him subdued, we will interrogate him. Should we need to dispatch him the traditional way, we will do so. Without their leader and his undoubtedly personal reason for seeking Astrid …" Irma's teeth ground together, thinking of what those personal reasons might be. "Without him, his men should depart willingly."

"Oh!" Sister Grace's gasp expressed dismay. "You think …willingly?"

Alice whispered something to Grace that caused the younger woman to bow her head.

The other women seemed nonplussed themselves. For her part, Irma imagined Bjorn returned aboard his longboat, sailing away from her. Would he look back toward her as he left?

Her insides clenched.

Such foolishness was no doubt the dregs of the mysterious enchantment they suffered under. No matter. Soon, a memory was all he would be, and that was how events must sort out.

"One way or the other, they will go. So it must be." Mother Agnes folded her hands in front of her.

"So it must be," repeated Irma.

"But—" started Sister Alice, only to fall silent at a withering stare from the Mother Superior.

Alice firmed her lips and continued. "I must remind all of you that it is *not possible* for them to leave the island, willingly or not. Once here, we all remain."

"And that includes these barbarians?"

"That is what the texts suggest." Alice spoke to

Irma, though her gaze was on Sister Grace's bowed head. "If there is a way, I have not found it."

Irma rubbed her hands together thoughtfully. "First things first. We'll find Harald, and then we'll see if there's not some way after all to restore the island to its previous existence." She flexed her fingers in expectation of the battles to come.

Though she formed the mission clearly in her mind—things must go back as they had been, and the women must be alone again on the island—she could not help a traitorous twinge at the idea.

Such irrational feelings could be indulged later, she decided. For now, she had a hunt to begin. And she knew her quarry.

The Black King she had to corner was this Harald. Time to make the first move.

Chapter 7

"Sister Mary Irmengard, wait!"

Halfway down the spiraling stone staircase, Irma paused at the Oracle's voice. The other woman's footsteps were nearly silent. When Irma turned around, she noticed that, peculiarly, the island's Wise Woman was barefoot. Sister Catherine stopped on the step above Irma, putting the two of them at eye level. Her dark blue eyes, usually as still as the deepest ocean, sparked with uncertainty.

"Sister Catherine?" Irma said after a long pause, concern in her voice.

Seeming to remember herself, the dark-haired woman straightened her neck. "Yes, I—" Catherine appeared to struggle for how to begin. "—I hesitate to mention what may best be forgotten, but I recall from when you first arrived on the island that you were, let's say, not unfamiliar with barbarians of this sort."

Irma felt an irrational flare of irritation. "That was, as you say, a long time ago," she said in a quelling tone.

"Although it makes you uncomfortable to think about—"

Irma snapped forward on her heels and began walking down the narrow stairs again, leaving the other woman to trail behind.

"—you must see there's an advantage in your knowing the enemy, as it were." The other woman raised her voice as she trailed Irma down the stone steps. "You possess valuable insights that may help us determine how to …handle …these men."

Handle seemed a strange word to Irma, but she kept walking, trying not to stomp her booted feet as she went. She did not want to think about that time before.

"Alice, of course, encountered barbarian raids before but as a frightened girl. You, on the other hand …"

Irma paused on the last step and turned. "I was one of them. Is that what you mean?" She raised an eyebrow in challenge.

Again at eye level, Sister Catherine visibly steadied herself. "I do not mean to label you either a barbarian or—"

"Or?"

"Or suggest a lack of loyalty. I only—"

"You question my loyalty?" Irma hissed.

Sister Catherine straightened. "I do not. Indeed, I said the exact opposite. I *do not* question your loyalty, Sister Mary Irmengard."

Irma took a deep breath and expelled it in a long stream. "I hear you, Sister Catherine. I apologize for taking offense. This situation is—"

"Let us simply say it is unprecedented. I only wanted to suggest that you share with me, *with us*," she amended, "your knowledge of these men, how their bands operate, their …relationships."

"Relationships?" Irma tilted her head in question.

Sister Catherine appeared uncomfortable again. "As you know," she said pointedly, "a powerful magic has brought the barbarians and our sisters …together."

Irma rocked back on her booted heel. She took in

again Sister Catherine's disheveled appearance, her bare feet and head, her uncharacteristically distracted air. "Are you asking what I know about their *sexual* relationships?" She kept her voice carefully modulated.

The other woman flushed red. "I know that you—"

Slashing the air with the flat of her hand, Irma interrupted her. "That was many years ago, Sister Catherine. What I learned then is that you cannot put any faith in a man's loyalty to a woman, no matter what he says."

In disgust—whether at herself or Sister Catherine, she did not know—Irma walked out of the stairwell and into the side door of the Worship Chamber, which was thankfully now empty.

"When they wish to bind a woman to them, such men have fine words and finer physical forms." The man she thought of now was not the one for whom she'd transformed from woman to warrior all those years ago. Rather, he was the man for whom, only hours ago, she'd transformed herself from warrior back to tenderhearted woman. "And some of them certainly know how to use those assets to charm their way into a woman's heart."

Irma tightened her jaw at the reminder. For all his appeal, his flattery, his bold—absurd!—statements of commitment, Bjorn was likely as faithless as any other. She could not allow herself to be drawn in by words and her own weakness to tender connection and physical passion.

In front of the now-vacant altar, Irma turned to where Catherine had followed her. "Such men do not stay. They do not remain true. Their bodies, as well as their affections, are bound to roam. It is their nature." She forced a shrug that covered the sting of that hard-learned lesson.

At that moment, a strange vibration rumbled under and through the paved stone floor beneath their feet.

A second later, a fierce, warm wind blew through the Worship Chamber.

From the main entrance up the center aisle, the sudden gust of air swept along the pews to the front where the two women stood at the altar to the island goddess. Pages of an open text on the podium flipped and rustled chaotically. Irma crouched in a defensive pose, palming a dagger and looking for the source of the wild energy that had invaded the sacred space.

When her attention returned again to her sister, Irma rose up to full height. She stepped backward once, then again.

Sister Catherine's dark-blue robes billowed out around her body, blown by the wind. Her unbound hair lifted and swirled around her face. Her eyes had rolled back into her head. Irma would not have been surprised to see her float up off the floor, but for now her bare feet stayed on the ground.

The spirit was upon her.

No longer Sister Catherine, she was now, in full, the Oracle.

Hardly breathing, Irma kept herself motionless on the edge of the whirlwind. Its power tugged at the fine strands of her hair that had come loose from her braid. She had been in the presence of the Oracle before but only within the structured convent rituals of homage to their benevolent spirit.

This force was something new; it was a power to be respected.

Irma waited.

“Mary Irmengard, We so named thee, Divine Protector.” A voice deeper and more resonant than Sister Catherine’s, a voice that sounded like many voices, emerged from her mouth.

Irma’s jaw went slack. To be called upon, by name, by the Oracle! In stunned shock, she could only remain mute in the presence of such power.

“You guard this island well, and your sisters.”

“Th-thank you, Lady of the Island.” Irma’s words sounded faint amid the rushing wind. They lifted up and about and dwindled to nothing.

Though she knew she should have bowed, she could not take her eyes from the Oracle’s wind-tossed form.

“As you guard yourself,” that eerie voice continued. “You are also Mary, the bitter drop from the sea.”

Irma’s stomach dropped at the explanation of her name’s meaning.

“Let not lessons learned in youth harden the walls of your fortress,” the Oracle continued in a lilting, multivocal tone that vibrated through the vast room. “Look to the hearts of those who come. Today there are battles to fight, but not ones of blood. Tear down walls to build new ones. Tomorrow you shall need such might, as more will come and blood this time will flow.”

The wind surged again, pushing Irma back yet another step. Warm air streamed up and around Sister Catherine’s body, lifting her hair straight toward the ceiling, swirling at the high rafters above the altar, and then dissipating with a gusty sigh. The floor’s rumbles faded, and the room fell into a heavy silence.

The sisters’ eyes met, deep blue to emerald green.

Sister Catherine blinked several times and then, appearing to recover herself, smoothed her hair and clothing in a manner that suggested familiarity with such divine possession.

Irma found she could not form any thoughts, much less words, in the ensuing quiet stillness of the sacred chamber.

After several moments, having gathered herself, Sister Catherine said gently, "You have been honored by the goddess. She has sent you a message as directly as she can."

This time, Irma did bow, dropping her head at the weight of the goddess's charge. Catherine moved toward her so that they stood close together. The Oracle had spoken, and now Mary Irmengard would have to carry out Her will.

The loaded words swirled in her mind like the divine wind. *Tear down walls to build new ones. More will come and blood this time will flow.*

"But what does it—"

Catherine stayed her with a soft hand on her shoulder. "I cannot interpret the words for you. They belong to you. Take them in. Turn them over in your heart. Plant them as seeds so that, when the time is ripe, they will be ready to harvest."

She smiled at Irma in understanding. "I wish I could be more help," she added, sounding more like herself. Her expression turned troubled.

Irma exhaled in a steady, cleansing stream. "No, you are of course right, Sister Catherine. I shall think of what this means and hope to be ready."

Irma walked down the long aisle to the main door of the Worship Chamber. Turning at the door she said in a raised voice, "Many thanks, Sister Catherine. We will do what must be done. And we will do it together." Her last word reverberated in the high-ceilinged chamber.

Together. That was important, Irma knew. She felt it like she had the trembling of the floor beneath her feet moments ago. She could even, she imagined, feel another draft of air, this one a mere breeze, stir the hair at the base of her neck. Still, she knew she was missing crucial information. She did not yet see the entirety of what must be done.

Before she could turn back around, Catherine called out to her. "Irma." Her deep-blue gaze had fogged over. "She wants you to know." Catherine moistened her lips, as if searching for a correct way to translate the message. "As man joins woman, bear joins bear," she said at last. "She wants you to know that the bear from the river's mouth mates for life."

At Irma's hard look, Catherine lifted up her hands in a helpless gesture.

Irma turned on her heel. Marching out of the room, she muttered to herself. "Fortress walls and bears mating for life and more will come. Why can't she just speak directly? All right, all right." She aimed her words at the ceiling, not wanting to provoke the island's spirit. "I'll think about it," she grumbled.

Hearing voices in the main hall, she directed her steps there and spotted her top archers, Sister Veronique and Sister Agatha, coming through the front door, deep in a heated conversation.

When she called them to attention, the two women stopped immediately. "Sister Mary Irmengard!" Veronique looked relieved to have found her. "The men have breached the Abbey."

Irma struggled not to roll her eyes at this obvious statement. Bowing her head, she sought for an ounce of patience. "Yes." After a moment, she decided to get directly to the point. "They're after Astrid." She leveled a commanding finger at each woman. "As she remains in the building that houses the sick ward, I need you to stand guard across the field, one in front of the building, one at the garden access. The man after her is called Harald. Make sure that neither he nor any of the men gains entry."

The two women exchanged a meaningful glance and then, as one, turned to Irma and straightened. "We will do as you require," said Sister Veronique levelly.

"And try not to look as if you're on guard," Irma added. "We do not want to draw attention to the place where Astrid abides."

After a short pause, Irma barked, "Now!"

The two women hopped into action.

Irma trusted them to do what she'd ordered, she did. But she thought she might just make sure of it.

Irma was about to follow them when her gaze lit on the little chess board she'd set up in one corner. Curious, she walked toward it and noticed—

She stopped abruptly. Someone had moved one of the black pieces.

The game is on. Resolution filled her.

She moved another bone-white piece into play.

Chapter 8

Meanwhile, in a green pasture just behind the Abbey, Bjorn was annoyed to find himself at the center of a brawl among men he counted as friends.

He ducked to avoid the punch thrown at his head. "You miserable Jotun," his comrade Magnus growled.

Knowing that Magnus likely did not recognize him amid the red haze of physical conflict, Bjorn replied with a wordless bellow as he threw a fist into the other man's gut.

Odin's beard, Magnus's belly was like an iron plate. Bjorn shook out his hand.

"Stay out of it, Bjorn!" thundered Njal, the large man behind him. He reached over Bjorn's shoulder to shove back Magnus's head with the flat of his palm.

"I'm trying"—Bjorn gritted, panting—"to assist you, you ingrate!"

"We were doing well enough without you!" said Bo, the third man, impatiently.

Bjorn sidestepped Magnus when the enraged man aimed a fist at the side of his head. He and Magnus were well matched in battle, of a similar height and build. However, Magnus had an idiosyncrasy that, when provoked, gave him a distinct edge.

Though normally of a steady temper, Magnus was a berserker. Once something set him off—and gods knew what that might be—he destroyed everything in his path until his maddened rage subsided. It very often gave him the advantage but was a damned nuisance when his frenzy overtook him in a conflict within the band.

"Obviously, you were not doing well," he grunted, swinging at Magnus's jaw, "since you've provoked Magnus into a temper in the first place." Bjorn made to grab the berserker's fist, which had just missed connecting with Bjorn's nose, to twist his arm behind his back. But his rival pulled back sharply, then kicked out and knocked Bjorn backwards into Njal.

Fortunately, as the blond giant Njal was taller and wider than both Bjorn and Magnus, he formed a sturdy wall behind Bjorn. Thus, both men stayed on their feet, ready for Magnus's next attack. Bjorn found himself grateful that, for whatever reason, Magnus was not armed with weapons more dangerous than his fists and feet, which were, he reckoned, quite dangerous enough.

As a martial light sparked in Magnus's eye, Bjorn prepared himself to fend off another blow. Bo, also anticipating Magnus's next strike, flung himself bodily at Magnus from the side. Bo's head down, he plowed into the berserker's iron midsection, throwing him off-balance enough that the two toppled to the grass below. Though significantly shorter and more compact than any of the other three men engaged in this fistfight, Bo had spent a lifetime developing combat tactics that suited his size and stature. He was not a man to be underestimated. Bjorn had gladly fought alongside Bo many times.

Before the wrestling match on the ground could produce a victor, however, the two grappling men were shocked motionless by a large quantity of water splashing in a torrent over their heads and torsos.

As both men shook the water out of their faces,

Bjorn barked out a laugh.

Bo shouted in outrage. “By the gods, that’s cold!”

Though the large man on the ground said nothing, from his startled look, Magnus had been jolted out of his crazed temper.

“Why did you douse *me*? I was not the one in an insensible rage.” Bo shook the water from his short, spiky hair like a dog.

Satisfied that no more blows would be coming his way, Bjorn looked over to see who had had the presence of mind to halt the fight so masterfully and saw …

Ah, there she was. Everything within him stilled at the sight of her. It was Signus, Yrse—no, his Mary Irmengard, his Irma. Something clicked inside him now that she had returned to his presence. She was here, praise Mimir. For Bjorn, in this moment, all else ceased to exist.

A shaft of late-day sunlight suddenly radiated out from behind the clouds that had gathered in the sky. Glinting off Irma’s hair, it surrounded her in a glorious, fiery blaze. Unlike the battle gear she’d worn when he’d first seen her in the courtyard, she now wore a high-necked tunic that, if possible, emphasized even more the round swells of her breasts, the inward arch of her waist that curved back out again to womanly hips. Her long braid crossed over her shoulder, a vibrant red rope he’d like to grab onto. She was a beauty unmatched by any he had ever encountered.

His worshipful perusal turned again to humor when he noted the expression on that vivid countenance. Wooden bucket dangling from her hand, she wore an annoyed look that matched his own earlier frustration with his fellows.

"That's enough from you oafs," she said bracingly. "This island is a place of peace and respite. Control yourselves and be men." She muttered other words he could not catch. Given the derisive twist of her mouth, he thought she might be questioning their manhood, or at least their maturity.

And then she looked up.

Her emerald eyes met his browner-green ones and time seemed to stop.

Their gazes fixed upon one another, and a smile creased his eyes at the corners. "That was well done, my dear."

"*My dear?*" said Bo, on his feet now and wiping water off his face with his hands. "Is this one yours, then, Bjorn?"

Bjorn started to agree, but a flash in Irma's eyes had him pausing. Still, it wouldn't hurt to make his intentions clear. "If she'll have me." He feigned a meekness he did not feel. *She would be his, by the gods.*

The returning glint in her eye said she was not fooled.

"Oh, I remember her." Bo smirked at Irma. "From the courtyard. So that's why you didn't want to fight her. Had other plans, I see." The way Bo's gaze trailed over her form set Bjorn's teeth on edge. He braced himself to knock Bo down a peg, but Irma disarmed him with her response.

"So we meet again, *Minimus*," she said with a smirk of her own.

Bjorn's laugh boomed across the meadow. "Minimus, is it?" He crowed through his mirth. Laughter shook his frame, such that he had to bend over, hands on his knees. Straightening again after several moments and wiping his eyes, he remarked, “Aye, you’ve the right of it, fair warrior.”

Puffing up his chest, Bjorn indulged in some well-earned gloating. “Bo, you should know that she calls *me,*” he said with a flourish, “*Maximus.*”

Ah, his woman did him proud. He turned to Irma, approval in his gaze. “You are my match in all ways, my dear.” Though she rolled her eyes at him, he saw a small smile tugging at the corner of her mouth.

“We have one, as well.” Bo’s tone was boastful, but he also sounded a little uncertain. “A match,” he added, glancing at Njal.

“We?” Irma’s brows creased with a frown.

“Njal and I.” Bo’s face took on a dreamy cast. “A lovely bird called *Angelina.*” He drew out her name with a kind of reverence Bjorn recognized in his own feelings for his Irmengard.

“You *and—*” Irma’s stubborn look had returned. Her eyes darted between the two larger men.

“Njal is the dry one, my bride.” Bjorn pointed helpfully to the blond giant. “He and Bo are very close friends,” he added, knowing the two shared everything—even, he supposed, women. “The large, wet, dark one just now hauling himself off the ground is Magnus. *Usually* a sensible man.”

Irma took a deep breath, appearing to mentally adjust to the notion that the two close friends claimed one woman between them. With a small headshake, she turned her attention to the damp, dark-haired man who had just struggled to his feet. “This one. Magnus.” She placed her hands on her hips. “He went berserk.”

“That he did,” said Bjorn. “In his case, it’s rare, sometimes useful, but also occasionally unfortunate. I suppose you've seen that before."

She cut him a sharp look. "That I have. What set him off?"

"No idea!" He shrugged. "I interrupted these three in the middle of their fight, and Magnus was already in a temper." He could tell she thought he was an idiot for getting in the midst of their brawl, so he explained further. "Magnus is not easily restrained once he's gone berserk. I'm not sure even we three could have done it without your wise maneuver with the bucket. Have I commended you for your adroit action, beloved?"

"That you have." She seemed unimpressed with his flattery, which made him smile at her again. *A challenge, this one.* As to be expected of the one worthy of being his bride. She delighted him thoroughly.

"Where did you get the bucket, anyway?"

"You four were making such a ruckus, I could see you from the Abbey. I grabbed the watering pail for the dairy cows in anticipation of having to soak you like a pack of wild dogs."

She turned her attention to Njal and Bo. "So you two," her tone was brusque, commanding. "What did you do to provoke him?"

"Us?" Bo flattened his hand on his chest with an innocent look. "Not a thing!"

Njal pushed Bo's shoulder in reproach. "Bo teased him about his learned lady." His deep tones matched his giant size.

"Do not speak of Alice," Magnus said roughly.

Noticing Magnus's hands forming into fists, a hint of red creeping up his neck, Bjorn sought a change of subject. Irma must have noted the same signs of Magnus's renewed rage, though, because she beat him to it.

"You two should know," she said to Njal and Bo, "that Sister Angelina is cannier than she looks. Do not assume you've won her over. I would never bet against her. Even if the odds are two to one. She'll be leading you by the balls soon enough, I reckon. But only if she wants to."

An unspoken message passed between Njal and Bo.

"*And* she's the daughter of the Abbey's Mother Superior, a formidable woman who is even now working to eject you meatheads from the island. Don't rejoice in the spoils of your victory just yet."

The idea that the Abbey's leader was even now plotting against them did not faze Bjorn, but it spurred Bo and Njal into action. With a shared glance, the two made to leave, heading away from the Abbey instead of toward it.

"Wait!" Bjorn and Irma shouted the word at the same time.

Bo and Njal turned around again.

"I have a question for all of you," said Irma.

"As do I," added Bjorn. Irma slid an annoyed glance at Bjorn, which he pretended not to see.

"Well then?" prodded Bo impatiently.

"Where's Harald?"

Bjorn and Irma looked at each other in surprise. Again, they had said the same words simultaneously.

Looking for Harald, is she? He raised an eyebrow and glanced sideways to where she stood. He could see a similar calculation in her own expression.

The three other men looked at each other. Some bargain was being made among them that Bjorn couldn't begin to guess at.

"Music Chamber?" Bo's suggestion lacked conviction.

"No," Bjorn and Irma said at the same time. He waved a hand at her as if to say, *Let me handle this.*

Instead, she looked at Magnus. "You know. Tell me."

How she'd determined that Magnus knew where Harald was, Bjorn could not fathom, but the trapped look on Magnus's face told him she had deduced correctly.

Magnus didn't answer but turned and stalked the other way, back to the Abbey.

To Bjorn's surprise, Irma raced after Magnus, wooden bucket dangling from her hand. She darted in front of the large, dark man to force him to stop. The two exchanged words, and in the end, Magnus bowed his head, cast a look over his shoulder, and then veered off in a perpendicular direction that led—well, Bjorn did not know where it led, but it was not back to the Abbey.

Perhaps she'd warned him off this Alice, Magnus's "learned lady" as Bo had called her.

On the other hand, perhaps she'd gotten Harald's location from him. Somewhat belatedly, Bjorn caught up to her before she could leave him behind.

"Did he know where Harald is?"

"He said Harald had gone down into the cloisters," Irma replied speculatively. "But he was lying."

She set off instead away from the Abbey, toward a set of buildings a little way off in the distance. Bo and Njal were already disappearing over a hill in that same direction.

Bjorn fell in step beside her.

Far from being offended by the charge that one of his comrades had been lying, Bjorn judged it as astute.

"Magnus is Harald's brother. Though not always the most quick-witted, he is a loyal beast. And tight-lipped. You suspected he knew Harald's location," he recalled.

"Yes." She finally looked him in the eye. "I'm usually good at reading people." When Bjorn could not help his flashing grin, she scowled at him. *"Usually."*

His grin stayed in place.

After a beat her jewel-green stare sharpened. "You're also looking for Harald?"

"Of course."

"Why?"

Instead of answering her directly, he said curiously, "Why are you looking for him?"

"He's your band's leader."

"Yes, that's why I'm looking for him as well."

"But I'm looking for him so that I can make him leave."

"Ah, well, as to that, perhaps so am I."

Irma shot him a narrowed glare, rightfully suspicious. Bjorn laughed loudly. "Aye, lass, it's the truth."

They walked on for a few moments, wooden bucket swaying between them, the structures in the distance looming closer. He could make out two low buildings connected by an open walkway shaded by a vine-covered trellis.

"Eager to leave are you?" she said at last. There was a deceptively mild note in her voice.

"Not I." He moved slightly in front of her, halting her movement across the green field. "I would never leave you, Mary Irmengard. Not now that I've found you again." He willed her to believe the seriousness of his vow.

And it was a vow, one that echoed in the core of his very being.

Chapter 9

Irma stared at the man before her, startled by his change of tone. He was a man of some contrasts, she realized. Warm and good-humored, he nevertheless possessed a ruthless determination that was obvious, even knowing him such a short time as she had. He laughed easily but was no superficial twit full of jokes. Instead, he possessed a deep well of emotion, even a kind of poetic soul. She brushed aside the fanciful thought. His body displayed enormous physical strength, and yet he operated predominately by a well-honed intellect and a shrewd understanding of human nature. Despite being a barbarian, he seemed to have an internal code of decency she responded to instinctively.

Something within her balked at the thought. Was it instinctive? She narrowed her eyes at him.

He reminded her of someone, someone from long ago.

I would never leave you, Mary Irmengard. Not now that I've found you again.

"You know my name." Perhaps it was not the most important discovery she'd made, but it added to her suspicion.

"Ah." He scratched his beard guiltily. "I did manage to find out that information, yes. But Irma." He eased his body closer so that she could feel the heat radiating from his muscular form.

"Yes?" She refused to step back. She would confront this man, and she would not—absolutely *would not*—drown in those moss-brown eyes of his that twinkled somewhat familiarly.

Without thought, she raised her fingers to trace the crow's-feet on one side of his face, then the upper curve of his cheek above his beard.

"I have known you by another name, by other names," he murmured. His eyes met hers directly. Willing her to acknowledge …

Surprise lanced through her. She dropped her hand from him.

He had known her in another time? The time …before?

Irma searched Bjorn's eyes. "Wait, you said you had found me 'again.' What do you mean? Did I know—" She abruptly halted.

"*You.*" She finished in sudden recognition.

Memories that she'd been unconsciously holding at bay poured over her, shocking her much as the cold water from her bucket must have shocked the two battling men minutes ago.

A younger version of this man, in front of her in a longboat, showing her how to wield her sword, instructing her in chess.

Those eyes, the color of fertile ground and new life, warm and sparkling with mirth.

That voice, encouraging her, rallying her.

All when she was someone else.

She sucked in a sharp breath.

"Signus …" he said, clasping her upper arm in his large hand, calling her back into the present.

"No!" She yanked her arm from his grasp.

She remembered.

He was from the time before. He was *that* Bjorn, the one she had known as a fellow soldier. She remembered that he'd told her hours ago, at the peak of passion, his full name, Bjorn of Aarhus. He had been part of that band, the one she had joined to follow Svend the Unworthy when he had left on his adventures. She had wanted adventure, too, and had craved to prove to her young lover that she was a worthy companion. So she had joined another band, determined to follow him, dreaming of their moment of reunion.

She had been a fool.

And this man had known her then, as both a fool …and a man.

She could not begin to fathom the whims of fate that had brought them together again, and here, where she had reformed herself and where she had found the balance of warrior and woman within herself.

How galling that he had remembered before she had, even despite her having disguised herself in male attire the whole time they had known each other before.

"Did you recognize me right away?" She found herself unable to meet his eyes when she asked the question.

He drew up a hand to cup her chin, tipping it to force her to meet his gaze. "At some point in the courtyard battle …" His voice tapered off as if he'd become lost in thought.

He looked over her shoulder, remembering the events of the morning. "It's a strange thing to find oneself battling nothing but women." He grinned down at her. His thumb covered her lips when she opened them to reprimand him, then brushed over them, lulling her into listening. "I was trying to break through your lines, which were very tightly held—you've a good group of warriors behind you—when a bright flash of red caught my eye. I was drawn toward it, toward you. Then, as I stood there with Bo—Minimus!" He chuckled. "As we stood before you, you raised your sword, bared your teeth and—I knew. I just knew." His eyes trailed over her features. "You were Signus resurrected, but in delightfully female form." That endearing twinkle sparkled in his eyes.

He had remembered her as a warrior, then, she realized with satisfaction, and he recognized her as such.

But—the thought hit her with the force of a blow—he had not only known her as a man. He had not just been her comrade on the longboat, her friend and occasional mentor through those months of soldiering.

"You were there." Her jaw clenched as she remembered how she'd left the band on that final, awful day. She pulled away from him abruptly.

He had been there, at the scene of her humiliation in the village pub. He had not only witnessed it, *curse him*, but—"You restrained me." The words were an accusation. "Kept me from killing that jackanapes."

A rueful expression on his face, Bjorn scratched his beard again—that gesture now so familiar, not just from today but from her life before. "That I did, Signus. Though you did not kill him, you quite effectively unmanned him."

"Aye, but in doing so, I unmanned myself as well." Her mouth curved in self-mockery.

"You were never a man," Bjorn pointed out. "And you must know the sniveling idiot was simply no match for your strength and honor. He was not worthy of you."

Frustrated and angry—with him, with fate, with the goddess, with herself—Irma clenched the handle of the bucket and began walking again.

"Yes, I know that now, some fifteen years later." Her voice was laced with exasperation. "In truth, I knew it at once. He did not deserve me. I had lost myself utterly for him. No man is worth that."

She said it reflexively. Having come to that conclusion during the harrowing journey to the island, she had repeated it to herself over the long years of self-discovery.

Let not lessons learned in youth harden the walls of your fortress. The echo of the Oracle's admonishment rang in her ears. Irma shook it off. She would not lose herself again, not for any man.

She did not stop to wonder how her words might fall on the ears of the man with whom she'd so recently shared her body.

"You do not harbor feelings for him," Bjorn said carefully, keeping pace with her across the meadow. Though it was a statement, Irma heard the question in it.

She scoffed. "I have not given Svend a thought, except to vow not to make myself vulnerable again to the charms of a rotting knave." She threw him a challenging look.

Bjorn surprised her with another grin, a searing flash of white within his brown beard and mustache. "Then I am fortunate that none of the other men on this island have a chance with you, my swan."

Wrapping large fingers around her upper arm, he pulled her to a halt. "For me, there is none but you."

Before she could utter a protest, he quickly swooped his head downward to claim her lips with his, opening his mouth over hers in an expression of pent-up lust …and perhaps something else she sensed in his kiss as well, something more.

Strength fled from her. Within moments, her whole body dissolved into a pulsing liquidity.

The bucket fell noiselessly from her fingers into the fresh grass.

****

Irma could not help but indulge in Bjorn's embrace. She mentally shushed the nagging inner voice that cautioned her to beware. *Just a few minutes of this. Just another taste of this man. What could it hurt?*

Their tongues twined together in a sensual duel before she pulled back so that she could focus on that plump lower lip of his. It was like a delicious, ripe cherry. She licked it, then sucked it into her mouth, grazing it with her teeth as a low groan vibrated through his chest. Praise the goddess, he was fine.

His hands grasping her hips, he pulled her softening body into his, now rigid with desire.

Giving into the ache deep within her, Irma hoisted herself up against him, first lifting one leg around his waist, then throwing her arms around his shoulders. Finally, she lifted her other leg, climbing him until her center met his.

Both of them groaned in pleasure.

"By Gungnir, you've too many clothes on," he muttered against her cheek. Embracing this way, their eyes met on the same level. He turned his head, and the texture of his beard on her smooth cheek raised erotic gooseflesh all over her body.

Bouncing her once, twice, and then a third time—at which they moaned long and low in unison—he sought a more satisfying jointure for their sexual cores. Keeping one arm around his shoulders to anchor herself, Irma slithered the other down his chest to his firm waist and then around his back. Downward farther still.

Deliberately, she squeezed his muscled ass. He cried out against her neck as his hips jolted against her, rubbing the hard shaft between his legs against her leather-clad softness.

"Sweet Asgard." His words were a husky whisper in the shell of her ear. "Is there never a bed when we need one?"

Smiling saucily, Irma leaned back in his arms, which so confidently held up her curvaceous form. Ah, how she loved his easy strength. "Do you need a bed for this then, old man?" Her tone teased him even as she undulated her hips against his, grinding their sexes together. Delight flared within her when he gritted out another low sound of passion.

"Old man!" Bjorn choked out a pained laugh. "Between the cursed clothing, lack of privacy, and absence of a soft bed, young one …" He bounced her again on his hard cock. "I confess, I can't see a way to get inside you as I long to be."

She knew there was a bed proximate. In fact, there were several within the two-story building now just before them. They might have their pick.

But it was also where Astrid lay insensate.

Irma had, unthinking, led him right to where Harald's quest lay. She had wanted to reassure herself that Astrid was well-protected, that Harald had not yet found her. If Bjorn knew her location, would he betray the young woman to her pursuer?

Despite the sexual pull she felt toward this man,

despite their previous friendship, she did not yet know Bjorn's endgame. She could not endanger her sisters with her reckless indulgence in this man.

She sighed heavily and experienced its echo in his exhale against her temple.

Even as she tried to put emotional distance between them, he cuddled her closer, stroking his hand over her back, soothingly, persuasively.

He rested his forehead against hers, and the sweetness of the gesture touched her heart.

"I cannot divest you of this tantalizing tunic," he murmured, his mind still on seduction. "My hands appear to be well occupied already." To emphasize the point, he clutched those large paws of his where they held her, one at her hip, the other along her back.

She could not stop the whimper that escaped her.

As if to steal the sound from her, he captured her lips again with his own. Pulling at them, he shifted his head first one way, then the other, until the two of them were almost lazily undulating against each other where their bodies joined, rubbing and caressing and murmuring into each other's mouth with pleasure.

Just a little longer, just a little more, that voice in her head urged. Everything went silent for long moments as they enjoyed each other's bodies, breathed each other's breaths, prolonging the simmering sensuality of their embrace without building toward a peak.

A long while later, the hardest edge of passion faded, urgency abated, and a warm, sleepy feeling of well-being pervaded her limbs.

They pulled apart slowly, and Irma let herself look at him, really look at him for the first time since she'd realized who he was. A feeling stole through her that she almost didn't recognize. Warm and sparkling like the peak of an ocean wave in the summertime sun, filled with joy and promise. It was …affection.

Even through these long moments of their embrace, his arms did not seem to have grown tired of holding her up, she marveled.

Irma drew her palm to pet his bearded cheek. Though she'd teased him about his age, he had no gray in his brown, shaggy hair—not even in his beard. Her thumb stroked over it, the short brown hairs soft in one direction, prickly in the other.

She supposed he hadn't been that much older than she had been when they had soldiered together. Her beardlessness had undoubtedly made her appear younger. His face was more tanned than before, the lines around his eyes perhaps deeper. Her finger traced them on one side, from eye to temple. She found herself adoring those signs of his having lived and having had joys that made him smile often.

All the same, she knew that the ravages of time were not always kind.

"I'm not as young as I was." Irma knew a rare pang for her lost youth.

"Praise Baldr, and nor am I." His eyes searched hers, and then they crinkled again at the corners. "As you have so ruthlessly pointed out."

Irma sensed his gaze drifting over her in returned scrutiny. Remembering how he'd last seen her, tear streaked and foolish, she loosened her grip on him so that her body slid down his and her feet touched the ground once more.

They could not remain here, Irma reflected. If she separated from Bjorn, he would become suspicious about the two-story building and who might be within. And she wasn't at all sure she could separate from Bjorn. More importantly, at a visceral level, she did not want to.

Casting a glance around at the two-story building where Astrid lay, Irma was relieved to spy Sister Agatha leaning against one of the posts of the garden trellis, watching Irma and Bjorn curiously. When their gazes met, Agatha straightened, but Irma shook her head slightly.

Satisfied that Astrid was well guarded, Irma made to walk again, knowing Bjorn would follow. This time she headed toward the shore instead of the sick ward where Astrid lay. When Bjorn grabbed her hand, she merely gazed at their fingers entwined together and walked on.

Seeking to put distance between Bjorn and the woman the barbarians had come for, Irma led them toward the sea path. All the while, her mind turned over the revelation that Bjorn was here. His presence had forcibly brought together two parts of her life: before the island and after. She had no desire to return to that old self and quite liked who she had become. But maybe there was another Mary Irmengard to be built in the future. The thought of tearing down walls to build new ones swirled through her mind again.

It was true she and Bjorn were no longer young. The Oracle's warning not to let the lessons of youth harden her flashed through her. They were both different now, had both grown, lived.

They marched on side by side for long minutes, until finally they walked along a path that overlooked sea-washed boulders and turbulent waves far below.

Perhaps, she thought, as she took in the salt of the

sea air, just perhaps she should soften herself to this particular man. Let her fortress walls fall to him, Bjorn of Aarhus. Perhaps—

Another thought struck her motionless. Caught off balance, his hand pulled at hers to steady himself.

Bjorn of Aarhus. His name. It meant ….

"Bjorn." She let his name roll on her tongue. "Your name means bear."

"Aye." He cast a glance her way. "And weren't you, before you were Signus the swan, weren't you a bear yourself? Yrse?"

When she tugged at their joined hands, he merely squeezed back.

Indeed, her birth-name, Yrse, was yet another word for bear. She had worn it proudly as a child, as a sign of strength, warmth, and power. "You recall that name after all these years?" He had, she knew, only heard it during that most humiliating confrontation at the public inn.

"You're very memorable." He shot her a small smile. It was not full-blown, though. He seemed aware of her inner struggle, her unhappiness with him. "More memorable than mine, it seems." With that, his smile turned a little sad.

"As man joins woman," she repeated, her mind on Sister Catherine's last words to her in the Altar Room, "bear joins bear." She looked down at their hands, fingers twined together.

Bjorn bent his head, so he could see into her eyes. "What's this now?"

"The Oracle," Irma said vaguely. "And your name, Bjorn of Aarhus. It means—"

"Ah, well, yes, Aarhus is where I settled once I put my raiding days behind me."

"'The mouth of the river,'" Irma translated. Then she thought of what he'd said.

"Put your raiding days behind you!" Her voice incredulous, she looked around pointedly.

He barked out a boisterous laugh that had Irma surging into motion again along the path high above the sea.

"Yes, well, it's true. I had settled down for many years."

"When you say 'settled down,' " Irma ventured with feigned indifference, "did you have a …a family?"

As seconds lengthened into minutes without his answer, Irma's heart began to pound. The Oracle had said the bear from the river's mouth mated for life. Had he already done so? Had he left a lover behind? A wife? Perhaps he was not as free as he had claimed. The thumping of her heartbeat almost made it hard to hear when he finally did speak, but speak he did.

"I did marry, but—" He squeezed her hand when she jolted in his clasp. "Hang on now, wench," he chastised her. "Don't compare me to that sniveling lout in your youth." Then his expression turning sad, he shrugged his shoulders. "She died. Some six seasons past."

"Oh." Irma imbued that one syllable with sympathy. "I am sorry, Bjorn. So sorry."

"It was …difficult. She was a good woman."

Was there a story behind that statement? Complex emotions colored his simple words.

"Children?" she asked tentatively.

He merely shook his head, pressed his lips together in what she imagined was unspoken grief. "But I stayed in Aarhus, which was home by then. I had tired of roaming. Perhaps you won't believe this, but I had my own smithy."

"A blacksmith!" Irma smiled with delight at the idea.

"Aye, not a bad one at that." His humor returned, he threw her a side-glance. "I made a fair few swords, some of which I'm quite proud of. I'd given up my own swordsmanship for good. But then a few weeks ago, Harald came to the village—" He cut himself off.

"Go on, then," she urged. "What about Harald?"

He cast a calculating look down at her. "Now, my bride, do not test my honor in such a way."

Irritated, she tugged again where their hands joined, but he held her fast. "Just a minute, just a minute." His brow creased with thought. "Let me see what I might tell you."

They paced on a few more moments in silence, the only sound coming from a strong, cool ocean wind that buffeted them along the cliff face.

"It seems best to describe our purpose here as part of a battle between clans," he said finally. "Harald is a relatively new chief and thus vulnerable. He also disliked raiding." At Irma's disbelieving glance, he lifted a hand palm up. "I swear by the gates of Asgard, it is true! Reports are that he missed the spring raids entirely the last two years. Much to the chagrin of some of his old band, he's talking of *irrigation* and such things."

"Why come here?" she prodded, annoyed he was not addressing the most obvious point. Would he tell her about Harald's obsession with Astrid?

Bjorn pondered the answer to her question. As they came upon a large, flat boulder, Irma brought them to a halt. Disengaging herself from Bjorn, she placed her hands behind her on the flat rock's sun-warmed surface and pulled herself into a sitting position upon it, a move developed over years of practice.

This was a favored place to watch the waves cresting against the rocks below and to observe the sun's setting on the western horizon. The wind lifted the small hairs that had escaped her braid as she waited for his answer, and it reminded her of the Oracle's exhortation.

Her bear stood before her.

Struggling to keep her walls lowered enough for him to scale, she made herself wait.

"I am Harald's friend, my dear." His voice was gentle with apology. "As he is mine. We met after I had tired of my raiding days, once I had settled down. To a quiet life, you know?" He cast her a wistful glance. "Harald and I have known each other for many years, though he lives in another village. We are bound by ties of loyalty and obligation. Though I had not gone raiding for many springs, when he called upon me some days ago, I could not say no." Bjorn ran a hand through his wind-tossed hair and wandered to the edge of the path, looking out over the sea. "As to his quest," he continued, "he is not a bad man. A great wrong was done to him. Another stole from him. Some …thing—something precious to him."

"Astrid." It was time to put all of their pieces on the board. Though she thought the young woman's name might have been lost in the billowing wind, his reaction told her that he had caught it.

He jerked his head back to her, focusing his eyes intently on hers. "You know her?"

Aware that he would see through it, Irma nevertheless gave him a half-truth. "I know that he searches for her here. But why?"

Bjorn turned his attention to the roiling waves again. He huffed out a laugh. “He had a vision.”

“A vision!”

“Of this island.” Bjorn stretched his arms out to encompass the rocky shore. “He said a voice had called him to come, that he would find Astrid on an island—what was it he said?—‘shrouded in a sea mist.’ I do not exactly recall. I confess that I thought he had—” Scratching his beard, he shot her a rueful look. “I do not hold much stock in prophetic foolery. And he was not …entirely …himself.” Bjorn sighed heavily. “But he was determined, and I thought perhaps I could be of use to him, my old friend.” Still staring out to sea, he added, “There was not much to keep me in Aarhus, and so I came along with Harald’s band, who are, I will say, not a bad group of men, all told.”

“My water bucket says otherwise,” Irma replied tartly. However, she could see that perhaps he was correct. Although they had fought—with the nuns as well as among themselves—she had not witnessed fiendish or brutal behavior from any of them. She frowned. That was a puzzle, given what she knew about barbarians from her own experience as one.

Swiveling toward the sea on her rocky perch, Irma gazed into the distance with Bjorn. “This vision,” she started, after long moments stretched between them. “Or, a voice, was it? What else do you remember of it?”

“Ah, lass.” Bjorn climbed atop the boulder to sit beside her. “I confess that I gave it no credence at all, so I don’t remember more.” He gave her a considering glance. “Does it matter?”

“As you’ve no doubt noted,” she pointed out, “you did indeed find an island ‘shrouded in a sea mist.’ And more than that, we've not seen men on this island in the twenty years it's been inhabited. At least"—she sent him a sharp look—"no men who could not be immediately *dispatched.* So I wondered if there was some divine …mischief …involved."

Assessing what she knew and what she had experienced directly, Irma could not help but think that the events of this day had been divinely orchestrated. But who was behind it? The benevolent spirit of the island or some other spirit who had called Harald to them, allowed his men to invade the Abbey?

"Bah!" She huffed in frustration. "All these spirits! I'd rather deal in that which is tangible, what I can hold in my hand."

Bjorn laughed and nodded. He brushed his shoulder against hers in a friendly way. "We are alike in that sense."

"We are alike in many senses," Irma conceded without hesitation. She allowed herself to lean against Bjorn's shoulder. In response, he stretched out a hand behind her so that she was enclosed in the shelter of his body.

Irma reflected on her concession. It occurred to her that they had begun in disguise to one another, hiding their true natures. In her life before, she had appeared to him as a man. Here on the island, even without his badger's mud mask, she had taken a long time to recognize him. They now saw each other more clearly. Indeed, although there was still much she did not know about Bjorn of Aarhus, she could envision that perhaps someday she would be her fullest self with him. Warrior, leader, comrade, partner, lover, woman.

They sat companionably on the rock, facing the sea

together as the sun turned clouds to brilliant oranges, reds, and pinks in the evening sky.

Important questions loomed in Irma's mind. What would Bjorn do to help Harald retrieve Astrid? Would they find themselves in battle against one another again? And then there were the things left unsaid about his years of "settling down." They seemed likely to continue on opposite sides of this conflict between man and woman, barbarian and nun.

It was unclear what the future held. Even the Oracle's statements were clear as mud to her. Yet some part of Irma, perhaps the girlish, dreamy part of her she'd silenced for so long, allowed her to put those questions aside and to enjoy this moment with the man who was, she knew, her lover.

Bear joins bear. Perhaps.

Chapter 10

Some while later, as the last fiery glint of the sun disappeared from the horizon, Irma sniffed at the air. "I think a storm may be on its way."

"Is that based on tangible proof?" Bjorn teased her.

"Many years of living on this island," she returned. With some reluctance, she eased out from the shelter of Bjorn's body and climbed down from the rock. "A scent coming off the sea. Note those quickly moving clouds." She pointed toward the east where, even in the twilight, sky darkened clouds were coming into view. "It'll hit the island before too long."

"How did you end up here, Mary Irmengard?" he asked curiously, following her.

After a second of indecision about where to lead him, especially given the impending storm, she set off again on the sea path along the cliff, away from the Abbey.

"Once you hoisted me out of the public house, you mean?"

"Is that where it started then?"

"It is. I …I knew I couldn't return to the band—"

He made a sound of protest.

"You think they'd have accepted me back in? After all that?"

He grabbed at her hand and swung it between them as they loped along the path.

"It's possible," he said. "We'd had women in our bands before."

"Had you?"

"Not many, but yes. Though, I will admit, none so comely as you."

"Right, right." She waved him off.

"It's not gallantry, Irma." He seemed puzzled by the way she'd dismissed his flattery. Before she could protest further, he continued. "Once revealed, you were very obviously, ah, a toothsome wench, as it were."

"Toothsome!"

He looked up as if remembering. "That hair, tumbling out of its braid. Those eyes sparking with feminine ire." He slid her a glance. "I admit that, when I lifted you up, I could tell—ah—you possessed generous feminine charms."

She elbowed him in reproof. "You could not."

"Aye, that I could. I was sorry to see you go. I thought you might return. So did the others. You were well liked in general. I liked you." His eyes met hers directly. "Most of us were quite impressed with the way you'd unmanned that unworthy fellow of yours. You were a veritable tornado." Irma cast him a skeptical glance. "The men waited a week in that gods-forsaken village," he continued, "but we gave you up for lost after that."

As Irma contemplated that revelation, first one large, cold drop of rain and then another fell upon them. "From what I knew, I had no reason to think I'd be welcomed back into the band. And you know it would have been more difficult than what you suggest."

His shoulders shrugged as if in reluctant agreement.

"For a while I simply …ran." She remembered that

long night, running, directionless, hopeless, bereft. “I found myself at a dock where there was a small boat and, well, I took it.” As part of a raiding band, she was no stranger to opportunistic theft.

“Where were you going?”

It was her turn to shrug. “I had no plan. But—” Here she stopped and pointed a finger at him. “—and no wisecracks from you—I thought I heard a kind of …”

“Don’t tell me you heard a voice!”

She shoved his shoulder. With the rain falling more steadily, she set off in motion again along the cliff path. “It was, though. It was like …some entity called me toward the sea. Could have been a voice, but it was more like …a feeling.” She shook off the memory. “A few sunrises and sunsets later, and here I was on Adytum.”

“Adytum?” he asked, puzzled.

“The name of our island,” she answered. “It means ‘refuge,’ and that is what it is.”

“And you’ve been here all that time?”

“That I have. When I first arrived, there were fewer of us. I think the Mother Superior was the first to come, perhaps more than twenty seasons ago, with her small daughter, Angelina.”

“It can’t have been easy, living out here in a small community by yourselves.”

“Surprised that a group of women could make it on their own?” There was challenge in her tone.

“Not at all!” His denial was hasty. “But to build such fortifications, not to mention planting crops, tending animals or hunting, making clothing and candles and soap! How do you do it?”

“We women are quite capable,” she reminded him. But, reflecting that he was not wrong to think it was more than their small group could have forged themselves, she added, "And the island provides."

"The island—?" he started, bemused.

A flash lit up the sky behind them.

"This rain came cursed fast!" Bjorn complained.

"That is the way of it here."

"Though I would follow you anywhere, my dear," he yelled over the pounding rain, "I do hope you're leading us to shelter."

She curved her lips in a smile at this, for indeed she did have a shelter in mind. But she decided to tease him. "Now why would I harbor the enemy?"

The corresponding rumble of thunder underlined her words and gave them an unexpectedly sinister edge.

"The enemy?" Despite the cold rain now bearing relentlessly down upon them, Bjorn pulled her to a halt, and she saw he was not amused. "By Mimir's head, lass, I am not your enemy!"

As she scanned his face, dripping with wet, she saw that his outrage covered another emotion. Was it …hurt? Her insides clenched at the thought. There was much still to be decided between them, it was true. But she could truthfully ease his mind on this point.

Reaching up, she brushed a hank of wet hair off his forehead. She combed his hair with her fingernails, and his eyes went to half-mast. "You are not my enemy. I do know that." She let her palm linger on his cheek. "Bjorn, I do." She lifted up and took his mouth in a hard, wet kiss.

Pulling away, she took his hand again. "Come," she said briskly, shaking the rain off her own face. "There is a shelter along here. Though not elaborate, it will do well enough."

She broke into a run, and without another word he matched her pace. Turning off the path, Irma dragged him farther along until they stood in a grove of trees. Even with just the newest budding leaves of early spring, the canopy kept the worst of the torrential rain off of them. It was quieter here.

A few yards later, a small thatch-roofed cottage made of stone came into view.

Circling the modest structure, Bjorn tapped on a wooden shutter which remained shut fast. "Appears abandoned."

"No, just not currently in use," she amended with a smile. "The island provides."

****

With a practiced move, Irma jostled the handle to the cottage door. It opened with a loud creak.

As expected, the interior was dark. The scent of earth and dried flowers wafted from the interior to tickle her nose. Leading the way in, she lit a lantern to reveal the cozy interior.

The one-room hideaway was as it always was. A stone fireplace held an iron kettle poised on a hook above the unlit hearth. A wooden rocker sat in the nearest corner, beside two shuttered windows. Decorated with elaborate carvings of flowers and leaves, a narrow bed frame lay tucked along the far wall, along with a thin mattress turned on its side.

Most importantly, it was dry.

And they were alone.

"We call this cottage the Hermitage. It is used for those who seek a short-term retreat from Adytum Abbey." Irma watched as Bjorn ducked his head to enter the small space. She rummaged through a large trunk just beyond the doorway and brought out fresh linens with which to make the bed.

Silently, after circling once around the room, Bjorn returned to the fireplace to stack a few pieces of the wood from the pile to the left of the hearth. He found a flint along the mantel above and within minutes he had built a warm, crackling blaze. Having righted the linen-covered mattress in the decorated bed frame, Irma moved to stand beside him in front of the fire.

The sound of sheeting rain provided a muted backdrop.

They did not touch. Both regarded the flames leaping up around the stacked wood.

Anticipation lay thickly between them.

"Irma," he said, just as she said his name. Exchanging a laughing glance with her, he laid his big warm palm atop her crown.

"Please." He sought her agreement to him speaking first. At her nod he repeated, "Irma." Then, with a little mischief in his gaze, he added, "Mary Irmengard, Signus, Yrse." He bent slightly at the knees to look her straight in the eyes, serious now, his hand trailing down her wet braid. "Under all of your names, you are always yourself. Magnificent." She searched his eyes, seeing in them only honest admiration. "You are my perfect match, my Sigyn, my queen. I regret I did not know it all those years ago. But I bless whatever divine force or twist of fate or *voice* has brought us together again."

She stared up at him while his large hands slowly unraveled the damp tresses of her braid in the growing warmth of the cottage. "I know that you and I have competing loyalties at the moment," he continued. "I do not expect you to betray your friends, as I cannot betray mine. However—" He sharply tugged on one strand of hair. "Those loyalties do not compare to the devotion I have for you."

Irma lifted her chin. "Bjorn of Aarhus, you are a man of honor. As you were my friend before, you will be my friend and lover from this moment forward. You are right: I will not betray my friends, nor should you betray yours. But you also now belong to me." She reached up to run her hands through his shaggy mop of hair. She pulled his head to hers, until she was breathing his breath. "We will go forward together," she said against his mouth. *Together.* She remembered the word reverberating in the Worship Chamber. "I will trust in you, as you also trust in me."

His lips nibbled at hers. "There is an answer for us." He murmured his words between tiny kisses. "One that preserves our honor."

"There is?" She pulled back in sudden interest.

Resting his forehead against hers, he huffed out a laugh. "Do not rush me, my dear. I only know there is one, not what it is." He slid his nose against hers. "I expect we must find it together, for"—he looked her close in the eye—"I would be one with you."

"I would be one with you," she repeated.

In her heart, it seemed as though they had exchanged bridal vows.

Their pact—to join together but not to abandon their other loyalties—they sealed with an impassioned meeting of warm lips and agile, darting tongues. She explored his mouth with hers, pulled that cherry-like bottom lip of his between her teeth and then licked at it before slipping her tongue back into his mouth to taste that warm, dark cave.

Praise the goddess, he was delicious to her. She trailed her lips across his beard, down to the warm, bare skin of his neck, and licked his pulse point.

His groan of pleasure rumbled against her breasts, now crushed against his muscular chest. Those brawny arms surrounded her, pressing their damp bodies tightly as if to fuse them into one being.

In response, she tightened her fingers where they lay at his nape. Moving her other arm to his wide, strong back, she drew a palm along his spine and then lifted her knee to hitch her leg over his lean hip.

One of his hands swooped from her back to her hip to the leg that wrapped around him in a forceful caress. “Sweet Asgard, we’re finally in the presence of a bed.” His grateful statement was a hot murmur against her ear.

“And not too muddy to use it.” A bubble of joy caught in her throat.

“Not muddy, no. But you, my dear.” Bjorn tsked, looking down at her. “You are quite wet, I’m afraid.” The hand on her leg swept back up to her hip, and he ground his pelvis into hers.

“More than you know.” She flashed him a seductive smile before seizing his mouth with hers again.

This time their kiss was ravenous, bold, almost desperate. Their lips slanted against one another, teeth clashing. Impatient hands grasped at clothing, tearing shirt and tunic over their heads and pulling at their leather breeches. Sometimes they tore at their lover’s clothes, sometimes their own, in their race to bare themselves to each other.

Irma all the while slowly marched Bjorn backwards toward the narrow bed along the wall. She pulled herself from him, feeling his rapt stare on her naked bosom, her nipples peaking in the cool air. Then she shoved at him with both hands.

He fell for her, bending at the knees, naked back hitting the linen-covered mattress. She tugged hard at his trousers until they were around his knees, and then she straddled him where he lay on the bed. She smoothed her hands over his shoulders, to his hair-covered chest, following where the hair arrowed from his navel to his groin. Her eyes landed on the large, hard cock standing straight up between his legs.

Goddess be praised, he's hung like a bear, too.

She remembered how he had felt within her, hard and pulsing, and went nearly limp at the thought. Her hand closed over his shaft, pulling upward with a tight squeeze that produced a strangled sound from him, then running her thumb over the hot, damp tip of his desire. With her other hand, she reached below him to tease his sac in a gentle caress, reveling in the curses he emitted through gritted teeth.

His own hands made themselves busy yanking her pants over her hips. "For the love—of Baldr, these—mold you—like—a second skin!" He huffed in frustration, fumbling, fingers trembling in anticipation.

Finally, after much wiggling and swearing, finally, *finally*, she was bare to him as he was to her. The leather trousers caught her above the knee, but it was enough.

Lowering her center to him, she used her hand on his shaft to stimulate herself, rubbing him from her sensitive bud—*goddess, that felt good*—to the wet entrance to her sex and back again. She began undulating rhythmically, riding the waves of pleasure.

Her breasts dangled below her, the unbound weight of them an erotic pull in itself. But then he lifted up and took a pointed nipple into his mouth. He sucked strongly, almost too much so, and the pleasure-pain reached from the hot, moist pressure of his mouth all the way to her core. She cried out and clenched her hand around his shaft.

With an elaborate string of curses, Bjorn rolled them both over so that they were on their sides, facing each other. Her fingers lost their grip on his cock with the sudden motion, and so she trailed them instead around the taught skin of his hip to the round curve of his ass. The pressure of her trousers on her thighs kept her from lifting her leg over him, but he wedged himself firmly against her. The tensing of his gluteal muscles warned her a second before he thrust himself inside her.

Her head arched back on her neck. She called his name and clenched her core around him, and he swore again. When she relaxed her tight inner muscles, he pulled out, then pushed in again. In and out, over and over, never going deep but with each thrust stroking the top of his shaft against her rosebud. Steady, steady but powerful, those strokes were.

She kept her heavy-lidded eyes on his in the dim light of the cottage, wanting to see him, wanting him to see her.

The wave of pleasure rushed up over her without warning and then broke, striking her like the lightning that still lit the sky outside. Her mouth dropped open, the pleasure so great it seemed impossible even to scream with it. She arched backward with the joy of their union, hoping he could feel its power as she did. *I love him. This man, this man, he belongs to me.* The wonder of it pervaded her body and spirit. In a word, it was joy.

A moment later, Bjorn's brows drew down over his

eyes, his face creased in rapture. He gasped out her name and, pulling himself from her, stroked his cock along the crease of her sex once, again, a third time—causing her to cry out at the stimulation of her sensitive bud. At last he shouted wordlessly into the curve of her neck.

They lay there, panting, feeling the aftershocks of pleasure. She held his trembling body; he held her as she softened against him.

Irma stroked his back.

Bjorn nuzzled at her throat, cuddled her breast in his palm.

Eventually, the uncomfortable tightness of her trousers around her knees made Irma squirm in his arms.

Bjorn's gaze caught on her bouncing breasts, and he uttered a rumbling groan. "Praise Idunn's apples," he said against her ear. "Lass, you've the most magnificent bosoms I have ever seen. And if you do not stop moving them about in such a way, I cannot be responsible for my actions."

Even as he scraped his teeth against the upper slope of one breast as if to take a bite, Irma's laugh rumbled up through her chest. "My bear, you have more curses in you than any man I've ever known! Idunn's apples, indeed. Though I don't mind if you continue to indulge yourself with my apples, I cannot promise you immortality, as legend would have it."

"Aye, but as to that, you've more than apples here." He weighed her breast in his palm and pretended to consider. "Grapefruits, perhaps. Or, rather, melons. Coconuts?" He ended on a bark of laughter when she punched his shoulder with her fist, and they both shook with mirth.

After a contented silence, his expression became

serious again. “Irma, I do not know anything about spirits or the whims of the gods.” The hand at her breast reached up to cup her smooth cheek instead. “But what we have shared is a miracle of miracles. I’d hang for nine nights for you, my love. I’d cross the Bifrost to be at your side. Name it, Irma. Tell me how I might prove my worth to you.”

She combed her fingers through his damp hair. Lifting his head, she peered for a poignant moment into moss-green eyes that glinted in the firelight, uncertain how to put her longing into words.

He seemed to read her mind.

Looking directly into her eyes, he said simply, “I see you, my dear. All of you.”

Irma searched his eyes. Yes. That was what she most desired.

“I believe you.” Tears gathered in her eyes. He would not want less of her than what she was. He would want not only all her strength but also her fierce and tender feelings. “I believe you, Bjorn.”

Chapter 11

After another indulgent hour in each other's arms, they stirred from the bed. So that they could wash, Bjorn rose to gather rainwater that had collected in a pail Irma pointed out to him that sat outside, just beyond the thatched roof's overhang.

He kept his shirt off, placing it before the fire next to Irma's tunic to dry. It was still pouring rain, and he had some hopes of donning dry clothing when it came time to leave.

He also enjoyed puffing out his chest, to Irma's quite evident admiration, and strutted like a peacock until she broke into laughter. Ah, a sweet sound.

When he returned to the warm, dry interior of the cottage, pail in hand, shaking the cold drops of rain out of his hair, he was delighted to see that Irma had discovered a loaf of brown bread covered in cloth and a hunk of cheese.

"A veritable feast!"

To this declaration, she merely replied, "The island provides."

The island provides, indeed. He puzzled over the deceptively simple statement. They sat close together on a woolen rug before the hearth, she cross-legged, he turned toward her with one foot flat on the ground, knee raised. Playfully, they fed each other bread and cheese, licking, sucking, and biting at each other's fingers. All the while, a fragrant tea began to boil in the kettle above the flames.

The warm, domestic peace of the scene melted something within him that he had not realized had frozen solid. He could not remember the last time he had known such contentment, such a feeling of …home. In fact, he was quite sure he had never experienced such a thing. Not even in his short marriage. His short *first* marriage, he amended mentally.

"If the island provides," he said around a morsel of cheese he'd nipped from her fingers, "where are our rings?"

She looked at him with a furrowed brow.

"We've said our vows, consummated our union, in a proper bed, no less." He waggled his eyebrows. "I count us properly wed, my dear," he clarified more seriously, wanting to make sure she knew that, to him, she was now his bride in truth. Although it required some courage, he asked, "Don't you?"

He watched her expression carefully, realizing that he could read every emotion that chased across her countenance like passing clouds.

Her frown changed to contemplation and then to a warmth and tenderness that he hoped was love. "And that I do, Bjorn of Aarhus." A troubling thought seemed to occur to her. "Am I to be Irma of Aarhus, then?"

"Irma of—! Sweet Asgard, lass, there's no going back to Aarhus for me."

Irma's eyes searched his, and he could see she was reluctant to take his meaning.

Clasping each one of her hands—a woman's hands, to be sure, but also hands that worked and fought—he pressed his forehead to hers.

"You are Mary Irmengard of the island Adytum. This is your home, your realm, my queen. And so it has become my home as well, to defend and guard alongside you."

Irma pulled back on a gasp, a shimmer of tears in her eyes, one escaping down her cheek. "You would—" Her words cut off as she choked on a surge of emotion. She swallowed and began again. "You would remain on the island? With me?"

He wanted her laughing again, so he said archly, "Looking forward to being a smithy's wife, were you?" At her short huff of denial, he continued. "Well, and what would you do in Aarhus then? You, the Guardian General of Adytum. You belong here. And now, because you are here, I belong here also."

She nodded at him slowly. "You do," she whispered finally and squeezed his hands in hers in affirmation.

"I shall be Bjorn of Adytum!" he announced, and she laughed up at him.

"Bjorn of Adytum." She nodded. "I like it. You do belong here." Even in the joy of the moment, her words were sober and sure. "I feel it."

"As do I." He tilted his face so that his mouth took hers in a sweet kiss.

"And anyway," Irma added with watchful eyes. "You should know, no one ever leaves the island."

He sensed she was telling him something important, but his heart only heard what most mattered. He would stay. With her.

The elation of triumph filled his lungs.

"And so I say, *where are the rings?*" Tipping his head to the ceiling, he raised his voice as if asking for a divine response.

Though he was mostly joking, he caught himself pausing …just in case. When no ring fell from the ceiling, he dropped his head again. "Alas, I suppose there are limits to what the island will provide us." To his delight, Irma laughed. "But have no fear, my dear. As a metal smith, I can rectify this lack in short order."

A thoughtful expression came over her. "Now you mention it, Bjorn, despite our lack of a blacksmith in the convent, I do think there's a spot where you might set up shop."

"Do you now?" His voice was lazy, as he found it hard to care about such practicalities at the moment. He slid his finger down Irma's arm, raised her fingers to his lips, and drew one inside for a long suckle that had her inhaling sharply.

"It's quite close to the weapons cache," she added. But her eyes were going foggy.

He nibbled on the heel of her palm, tickled the tender underside of her wrist with his tongue.

"I expect to—consult with—you—on any …" She was truly breathless now.

"Yes, my dear?" he murmured against her skin.

"Any daggers or swords that"—she leaned into him now, her words hardly above a whisper—"that we need or …*want* …"

"Only the best sword for my warrior bride." He took her lips with his.

That was the last either of them said for quite a while.

****

Several hours later, Bjorn's eyes opened as he leapt into consciousness.

A silent, motionless survey told him that he

remained in bed with his bride, his body curled closely around her sweet form, his nose in the soft fiery mass of her hair, his arm around her waist, their knees tucked together.

The rain had ceased. Through the slats of the shuttered windows, he could only make out darkness. No birdsong as of yet.

It was not quite dawn.

Something had awoken him. A small sound…

There it was. A light crunching sound, like a boot on forest ground.

Someone was here.

With as much speed as he could muster without rousing Irma, he disengaged himself from her, pulled on his breeches and now-dry shirt, and hastened to the door. A door that, he only now realized, had no lock, no bolt at all. His lady lay vulnerable behind him. A surge of protective fury rose in a red-hot flush from his chest to his neck, cheeks, and forehead.

Standing to the side of the door, he peered through a break in one of the shutters but could see nothing through the darkness beyond. He had two choices. The first was a defensive approach. He could stay and meet whatever threat approached here, stand between it and Irma, who lay in well-earned repose behind him.

But Bjorn much preferred an offensive move against a likely threat, and so he chose his second option. He shoved his feet into his boots and stuffed his shirt into his trousers.

With a last glance at Irma, Bjorn eased open the door.

He stepped into a damp darkness. Quietly, he closed the door behind him.

For a moment, all he could hear was the drip of raindrops that had caught in the leaves above and only now fell to earth.

Bjorn didn't hear so much as sense when the other form entered the clearing in front of the cottage. He knew he was no longer alone in the dark.

Moving swiftly in hopes of surprising their visitor, Bjorn threw himself in the direction of the forest path. His body slammed into another. He heard an object drop from the man's hand to land heavily on the wet ground beneath.

Immediately, he knew the intruder was another man, and his protective fury rose again within him. As they grappled together, unable to see one another in the heavy pre-dawn, Bjorn knew he had the advantage of both surprise and weight. The other man was agile, however, and slippery. They wrestled in silence until, finally, Bjorn had the other man's neck in the crook of his elbow and his arm behind his back.

"State your name!" he growled into the other man's ear.

"Thor's hammer, is that you, Bjorn?" gasped the intruder.

Bjorn loosened his grip but did not drop it. "Andor?"

"Yes, what are you—"

"No." Bjorn cut the other man off, tightening his hold slightly. Andor was a good man, and though he could clearly fight well, he was not a hothead like some of the others. Still, no one was to be trusted in such proximity to Irma. "You tell me, Andor. What brings you here?"

"By the gods, has everyone gone mad on this island?" Andor said in pained bemusement. "Bjorn, it is only me. It's Andor," he repeated, and Bjorn could tell he was intentionally leveling his tone. "Bard of the fleet. I carved those chess pieces for you all those years ago. You know me. Release me and let us speak as men, as brothers."

Bjorn heard the reason in his comrade's words.

"Very well." Bjorn dropped his hold on the other man. "But not here."

Bjorn headed away from the cottage, instinctively pulling a potential threat from his lady-love.

"Walk with me," he said impatiently, when Andor stood there, rubbing at his wrist.

The other man's shadowed form turned briefly toward the cottage where traces of yellow firelight bled from in between the cracks in the shutters. "Can we not—?"

"No." Bjorn's denial was firm. "Walk with me."

Andor sighed audibly, but then he stepped toward Bjorn. He paused, and in the darkness Bjorn could see his form stoop to pick an object off the ground.

"What is that?" He braced himself for an attack.

"It's a—" Andor paused, and Bjorn thought it might be from embarrassment. "It's an instrument." Images of weaponry, instruments of war, flashed through Bjorn's mind, and he grabbed Andor's wrist again. "Not a weapon, Bjorn." Andor's voice held exasperation. "It's a …a musical instrument."

"A musical—?" Bjorn said. But a glance at the cottage had him dropping Andor's wrist and proceeding into the forest. A few seconds later, Andor followed. They walked in silence until the sound of waves rising and cresting indicated that they neared the sea path along the cliffs.

As the path widened, Andor came abreast Bjorn so that they walked side by side. Bjorn glanced at him, "What brought you this way, Andor? And with"—he gestured to the large object that swung at Andor's side—"that."

Andor sighed heavily again in the darkness. "Frances," he said mournfully.

Bjorn halted on the path.

They had just cleared the trees, and the slim crescent of a moon in the sky allowed him to see the other man more distinctly.

"Ah." Comprehension filled him. "You have lost your woman."

"Sister Frances Ignatius," Andor affirmed. "She is …a goddess, my Freya, my Free Fire."

"And this?" Bjorn gestured at the object that he could now see was a large brass horn.

"I discovered Frances in the Music Chamber. She is music herself." His gaze took on a besotted look. "But Harald made to attack her—"

"Harald!" said Bjorn in surprise. "Attack a woman?"

Andor dragged a hand through damp strands that suggested he'd been out in the rainstorm. "He was mad with rage, Bjorn. I've never seen him like that. He told Frances about Astrid, demanded she show him where they've hidden her."

Bjorn's attention sharpened. "And did she?"

"No!" said Andor. "And I—in truth, Bjorn," Andor added, his voice troubled, "I don't know that I trust him with such information. Frances denied that Astrid is here, but it seems likely—"

"Aye, she must be here." Bjorn had come to that

conclusion himself. He set off eastward along the path again. "And the nuns now know she is the target of Harald's quest. They seek to protect her."

Andor caught up with him. "I cannot help but think …" Andor paused cautiously. With a quick glance at Bjorn, he continued. "I think that perhaps they are right to do so." As if expecting a reprimand, Andor hurried on, "You know, Bjorn, that I am loyal to Harald, that I know the rightness of his intentions."

"But you feel, in this state, he cannot be fully trusted."

In the faint light of dawn appearing over the eastern horizon, Bjorn could see Andor nod.

"Did Harald …" Bjorn hesitated, searching for the right words. "Is your lady, Frances—is she well?"

"I do not know. That is, I managed to subdue Harald."

"Did you now? That was no mean feat." Bjorn acknowledged Andor's statement with some admiration. Harald had not become chieftain without defending himself from many serious challengers. But then, Bjorn knew that Andor could also hold his own when needed.

Andor shrugged. "As I say, he was full of rage instead of sense. I could use that against him. It allowed Frances to escape."

Andor gave a rueful laugh. "As to this?" He hefted the horn. "I know I said it was not a weapon of war, but I did use it to knock Harald unconscious." His voice turned distraught. "Frances escaped, but when I went to look for her …" Andor halted on the path. "She has vanished. No one seems to have seen her, and I fear …I fear …"

Bjorn put a hand on the other man's shoulder.

"Andor, you know I am not a ...pious sort of fellow." And wasn't that an understatement? At Andor's quizzical look, Bjorn merely patted his shoulder. "But this island ..." He looked around at the lightening sky, toward the rocky cliffs and the waves surging below. "I do not believe that Frances will have come to any harm."

"Bjorn, did you—?" Andor glanced over his shoulder toward the direction in which the cottage lay.

Bjorn shot him a guarded look, his protective instincts coming to the surface once more. "Your Frances is not in the cottage," he said at last. "Continue your search ...elsewhere."

Andor's expression hardened for a moment, but then he nodded respectfully. Though Bjorn was the elder of the two of them, among warrior bands the measure of authority depended on a variety of qualities. Bjorn was not too modest to know that he possessed many of them. He knew that Andor had weighed his words, found them truthful, because of those traits.

Andor hefted the horn at his side. "I suppose I must keep searching, then." Before heading back east, toward the Abbey, Andor paused again. "Bjorn, you don't think that this, this island and—" He swallowed before continuing. "—our *experiences* here. These women ...It's not some ...enchantment." His voice was uncertain. "Is it?"

Bjorn considered the possibility seriously. It had occurred to him, hadn't it? But then he thought of his Mary Irmengard, a woman of his past who had returned to him. He did not doubt the strength of their bond. "I do believe there is some enchantment here," he said at last. "But that is not all that it is." He smiled at the other man and slapped him heartily on the back. "I wish you luck with your Frances."

Andor flashed a ghost of a smile back at him. "And you with your lady." With a short nod, he walked toward the Abbey, leaving Bjorn standing on the cliff path, watching him go.

Though it seemed a bit unkind given Andor's evident misery, Bjorn knew a surge of satisfaction that, unlike the other man, he needed no luck with his lady.

She was his already, fully, and in truth. A smug smile tugged at his lips.

Turning on his heel, he set off westward along the path, back to the cottage.

But a few feet along, a glint down among the jagged rocks below caught his eye. Curious, Bjorn stooped where he was and squinted, but still he could not make out what the sun's fragile first rays had lit up. He set his booted feet off the path, bracing himself on the edge of the cliff. Hands on his knees, he peered down. Astonishment struck him and a surge of laughter bubbled upward from his belly to ring out across the rocky shore.

By the goddess, the island does provide. Bjorn directed his mirth skyward in appreciation. He wondered how he might claim his prize and knew with sudden clarity that he would need Irma's cleverness and experience. And after all, it was her prize as well. He imagined the look on her face when she saw it and chuckled again.

Intending to return to the cottage, he shifted his weight to the path.

But just then, without any warning, the edge of the cliff, softened by the heavy rains, crumbled under his booted feet.

Unmoored and unbalanced, Bjorn scrambled for a

hold among the rocks, first for his feet, and then, as the rocks dropped from under him, for his hands.

It was no use.

Without another sound, Bjorn fell and fell, landing in a heap on the rocks below. For one more second, his hands clutched and grabbed at the small rocks that fell around him, but then he stilled. The hints of light in the dawn sky darkened in his vision as he blinked upward, gasping and then—

Nothing.

Bjorn of Adytum's body lay sprawled among the rocks midway down the cliff. Motionless.

Chapter 12

A chill in the air roused Irma from a deep and pleasant sleep. She came awake slowly, stretching her limbs with her eyes closed, taking in the delicious aches of being well loved.

Listen first. The old routine of hers began.

Hearing nothing, with a contented sigh, she opened her eyes.

Surveil surroundings. Assess threats.

It didn't take her long to realize that she was alone.

Contentment fleeing, she sat up on the mattress, the cool air pricking her flesh. The fire had burned down in the hearth, now nothing more than ash. Morning light peeked through the closed shutters on the cottage windows. Hastily, Irma grabbed her tunic from where it sat by the fireplace—and she noted that Bjorn's shirt no longer rested beside it.

Reason assured her that he had likely gone out to relieve nature's call or to gather more water or …something.

But as she dressed, she couldn't shake a feeling of dread. The cottage was so quiet, so empty without him.

Which was a ridiculous thought.

Irma tapped herself lightly on the cheek to keep herself in the present. Picking up a hunk of bread, she took a large bite. She observed that he'd left without breaking his fast. Given the size of his appetites, that did not bode well.

When he didn't come through the door after another few minutes, she wrapped the remainder of the bread and cheese in their cloth and tucked them in a small sack that sat on a hook by the door. Upon meeting up with him, they could share what was left over from last night's simple meal. Stepping into her boots, Irma cast one more glance around the cottage and opened the door.

She was greeted by the damp scent of the forest after an evening's rain and the cheerful noise of birds calling to each other among the trees. Her ears didn't pick up any other sounds, certainly no sign of Bjorn, but she circled the cottage anyway, just in case.

Expanding her circles gradually, she trained her eyes on the ground and was rewarded when she saw an area in which the forest brush had been disturbed.

The rain hadn't washed away the signs. That indicated the confrontation had occurred once the rain had stopped, thus in the early morning hours. At least that would make for convenient tracking.

Narrowing her eyes, Irma crouched down to investigate. Some sort of scuffle, she determined, noting the heavy circle of one bootprint and then another of slightly different shape, narrower. The length and depths of the prints told her both parties were men. Some large object had pressed down the grass beside the struggle, but she couldn't guess what.

Irma shook her head in irritation. It seemed as though someone had found the cottage and Bjorn had—*goddess love a foolish man*—set about dealing with it himself while she lay obliviously in bed. Safe.

Men.

She breathed out her frustration and forced herself

to embrace the cool clarity of reason.

Standing, Irma followed the trail to the forest path. Though the smoothness of the path made it harder to discern where the skirmishers had gone—one of whom, she presumed, was Bjorn—logic dictated that they had kept to the path.

And so Irma walked the path, eyes open for signs that men had passed there in the last few hours. Here was a broken twig, there a scuff in the wet sand along the path. There were only two people, she decided, the one with narrower boots and the one with wider ones. They did not appear to be at odds, rather walking side by side, occasionally pausing and then moving on again. Irma steadily tracked the pair, increasingly convinced they had simply followed the path. At least that made her job easy.

But then, just beside the large boulder on which she and Bjorn had watched the sunset yesterday, the signs changed. Although she discerned the marks of one man's boot tracks, the other was no longer with him, she decided.

Irma peered into the distance, seeing signs of no one.

Whoever the second man had been, he was long gone.

Puzzled, she crossed her arms over her chest, leaned back against the boulder, and gazed sightlessly at the ground. More than puzzled, she was …worried.

The two had started in a brawl. Bjorn was undoubtedly protecting the cottage. Perhaps it had been too dark to see who he was fighting at first. Yet it appeared that, once they left the forest, Bjorn and the other man had walked together as companions, equals. There were no further signs of a struggle.

At this spot on the path, Irma deduced, just beyond the large flat rock she leaned on now, Narrow Boots had proceeded eastward along the path, toward the Abbey. Wide Boots—and given Bjorn's size, she thought it logical to assume that was Bjorn—had not followed. He should have returned to the cottage, to her. But her tracking to this point had not shown bootprints headed back in that direction, only the one pair moving eastward.

Where else might he have gone?

She took a few steps toward the meadow, where the building that held the sick ward lay. Then she stopped, the cliff's contours in her mind's eye.

Slowly, she turned back so that she gazed out at the gently rolling ocean waves, calm but full after the storm.

Her eyes trailed the cliff's edge. The first path revealed nothing unusual, the rocky boundry worn smooth by the elements. But then, her eyes passing again over the view out to sea, she noticed a ragged indentation that looked like someone had taken a bite out of the path's edge. Carefully, she eased forward. Testing the ground with her toe before putting her weight on her foot, Irma crept from the path.

Yes, just there, the ground appeared to have broken away. Irma bent to run a finger over the jagged rock that remained. The break was raw and dry, drier than what surrounded it, and so the collapse had happened after the rains.

Irma's heart pounded rapidly, heavily in her chest and ears, drowning out even the sound of the waves crashing below. She forced herself to take a cleansing breath, exhaling slowly. Uncertain of the terrain's stability, she lay down on the ground to distribute her body weight and edged out, inch by inch, over the cliff’s steep drop.

At first, she saw nothing but the rocky incline that went down in narrow terraces to the sea.

She shifted slightly, first this way, next that way, until an unusual shape caught her eye, and then—

“Bjorn!” she gasped. Then louder, “*Bjorn.*”

Her voice rang out over the cliffs.

Two more times, she called out to him.

But he did not answer.

The shape, on which now she could make out tousled brown hair and tanned flesh, lay still.

Irma inhaled and exhaled slowly to calm the panic that threatened to steal her wits. Her concentration focused like a sharp blade on the task at hand. She had not found him to lose him so quickly.

Surveying the descent to the rocks below, Irma could see no easy way to reach him where his body lay motionless on one of the flat boulders halfway down to the shore.

Very well, she could not do this alone.

She eased backward toward the cliff path, rolled back onto her feet, and headed in the direction of Narrow Boots, back toward the Abbey.

Bjorn would be all right. He had to be.

She would need all the help she could get.

Irma broke into a run.

****

“Watch it! Not so close to the edge!” Bo shouted.

“Howm’I to get the rope angled properly if I don’t, then?” Njal turned to his friend in exasperation.

Bo shoved him aside. “Let me do it. I’ve less mass to send the whole thing crumbling into the sea again.”

Irma focused on the bustling activity around her, trying in vain not to think about Bjorn's body lying halfway down the escarpment that led to the roiling sea below.

She had run all the way back to the Abbey.

Before anyone else, Irma had encountered Bo and Njal with Angelina in the main hall. Through heaving gasps, she had explained what she believed had happened and what she needed now to rescue Bjorn.

During her seemingly endless run back to the Abbey, Irma's mind had whirled and looped in circles, trying to think of what to do. She must get to him. She must. Although Irma had recovered many women who had landed or washed up on the island in a variety of ways and places, she had never encountered such a challenge as this. Not only was he stranded below a cliff face that had already proven unstable, his size and unconscious state would make it nearly impossible to move him to higher ground. These facts turned and turned in her mind.

And then those loops in her mind had become visible to her, and she suddenly knew what to do.

"Angelina," she had said in the main hall. "Do you remember last year, we had a vessel full of crates wash up on the southern shore?" Such unexpected shipments of valuable supplies were not unusual. Irma knew it was one of many ways the island provided for them all. However, in this case, the location on the rocky southern cliffs had forced them to use their ingenuity. "We used a pulley system to raise them."

"Yes!" Sister Angelina had brightened as she recalled the incident. "We returned the items to storage in the cloisters."

"Collect them, and don't leave anything behind." Irma snapped out the command.

Angelina had darted into action with admirable alacrity.

"And bring along any other sisters who can help us rebuild it!" she called to Angelina's back. At the other woman's acknowledging wave, Irma had given her next orders to Bo and Njal. They would need strong backs to hoist Bjorn's weight, even using the pulley system.

The two men had raced into motion to gather their fellows.

Irma had her own task to perform, swiping the thin mattress from her bedchamber. They would hook the pulley to the mattress, lower it down the cliff face, place him on it, and then—the part that most needed brute strength—lift the mattress back up.

Heading back into the main hall with the rolled up mattress strapped to her back, Irma's eyes had caught on the chess match she'd set up the previous day. Through a narrowed gaze she could see that her opponent had moved a piece, toppled one of her players.

"No." Her voice echoed in the empty hall. She pocketed the conquered piece and shifted one of her own in a strategic countermove.

Marching away from the game board and back toward the cliff path, Irma vowed she would not lose any of the battles she waged today.

And so now, what seemed an eternity later, a small, determined crowd gathered along the cliff path. Irma was directing a group of nuns putting together the pulley system they would use to haul Bjorn up the side of the cliff. The four of them together carefully knotted the thick hemp rope Angelina had commandeered. They looped it around the edge of the wooden spinning wheels they had modified last year for that purpose. Braced against the flat rock for stability and leverage, this basic machine would allow them to lift a man of Bjorn's weight up to the cliff path.

She hoped.

"Irma!" Bo's voice called her back to the moment. "Let's test the machine."

Irma nodded and returned to the nuns. Together with the men, they aligned the system so that the mattress would descend to the proper spot. When a smattering of rocks crumbled under him, even Bo was judged too heavy to navigate the cliff's edge. So little Sister Grace, the smallest person gathered with them, had nervously shimmied herself onto the edge, rope in hand, under the watchful eye of a silver-haired barbarian whose tight jaw expressed great displeasure at the risk she was taking.

Grace lowered the rope and shakily called out to them that it was in position before scampering back toward her barbarian protector who caught her up in his embrace.

"All right then," Irma said to the women and men stationed at the pulley. "Lower the pad by my count, and let's see if this works. One, two …"

With a smooth easy motion, those who stood with rope in hand let it out to Irma's rhythmic count.

"That's it." Bo observed the proceedings from atop the flat boulder.

Irma called a halt, then had the team raise the mattress again to a reverse count. With it back in its original position, Irma walked over to consult with Bo.

"I think that'll work." Bo brushed the dust from his hands. To Irma's surprise, his earlier cheek had veiled a serious resourcefulness. "But someone will have to go down first who can get him on that thing. And I wouldn't recommend going down the way Bjorn will come up." Bo eyed her, consideringly.

"Aye." She knew what he was thinking and had come to the same conclusion. "I'll do it but on a separate line. If we've a long enough coil of rope, we can tie it off on that tree over there." She pointed to a sturdy tree a few yards away from the path.

"Have you rappelled down these cliffs before?" Irma's irritation must have made itself visible because Bo raised his palms. "I ask," he explained, "because if you injure yourself in rescuing Bjorn, he will kick my ass."

An unexpected laugh burst from Irma's throat, but Bo's expression remained serious. "Yes, I've done it before," she assured him. "Who do you think hooked the crates to the pulley last year?"

Bo nodded at her and jumped down from the boulder. "I'll count out the pace, then, when it's time for that." Quickly slipping into motion, he dashed inland. "Oy! Angelina!" he called. "Get us another rope, darling."

Chapter 13

Fortunately, not many minutes later—for Irma's impatience was in danger of overwhelming her good sense—Irma had positioned herself to climb down the cliff face.

Harnessed in by a thinner cord strapped around her torso, she firmly grasped between her hands the thick rope by which she would descend.

Irma drew in a breath, redolent of the bracing sea air, and blew it back out again in a steady stream.

"Ready?" Bo called to her from atop the boulder.

"Ready," Irma returned. Then slowly and carefully, she lowered herself down the cliff toward Bjorn.

Hand over hand, her boots carefully feeling out footholds in the rock, she descended, the sound of the waves growing louder in her ears.

"Almost there!" Bo's voice drifted down faintly from above.

To this point, Irma had avoided looking down so as not to disturb her balance and concentration, but now she peered beneath her and to the right. The slab of rock on which Bjorn's body lay was only a few feet below her now, almost in reach. With a few more careful steps downward, she dangled her foot over the rock, gently lowering her weight onto it.

As soon as she was on two feet, she unknotted the harness that tethered her to the thick rope and bent to her love.

Blinking the sweat from her eyes, Irma ran shaking hands over his form. Right away she noted that his chest moved shallowly as he drew air into his lungs. She bent to his ear and said his name.

He did not rouse.

"Here!" She called up to the cliff top. She couldn't hear anything in return over the sound of the sea, and so she wasn't sure if they had heard her. Turning her gaze upward, she saw Bo's arm come into view and wave in acknowledgement.

From where she was below, she could see the mattress begin its descent on the pulley rope.

In the meantime, Irma assessed Bjorn's injuries. She brushed the hair from his forehead tenderly. Feeling around the back of his head, she noted a large bump within hair matted with dried blood. The good news was that the blood was no longer flowing. Yet that also meant that the injury had occurred some time ago.

Gingerly, she probed around his neck. Though she knew it could be hard to tell such things, she could discern no injury there. More firmly, pressing along bone and tendons, she swept her hands along his shoulders and collarbones, down his torso, then over the long, muscled arms. She straightened his legs once she'd assessed them as whole and unbroken. Though undoubtedly bruised, he was in one piece.

She exhaled in a gust of quiet relief.

And yet, he remained unconscious.

"Bjorn!" She called to him again, this time with a firm shake of his shoulder. "For the love of the goddess, Bjorn, you come back to me!" Her voice was angry as she dashed the mix of tears and sweat from her skin.

Then she rained short, wet kisses on his face and neck, murmuring to him words of love. "Come back to me, come back to me."

The mattress hooked to the pulley rope was now at Irma's eye level, but she let the men and women above continue to lower it apace while she tended to her love. At last, the pad met the surface of the rock, and Irma turned aside to unhook it from the rope so that she could begin the work of maneuvering Bjorn's body onto it.

She froze at a soft sound.

"Irma?" It was only a whisper. Later she would think it impossible that she had heard it above the crashing waves.

She turned her head sharply and saw his eyelashes fluttering. "Bjorn!" Her hands again trailed over him desperately. "Bjorn, wake up! Wake up!" When her tears dropped onto his face, she used shaking fingers to wipe them away.

Finally, after what seemed like endless waiting, she saw him wet his lips, about to speak.

"Aye, lass," he whispered again almost soundlessly, a mere movement of lips. She let out a short whoop of joy that he was coming awake.

This time, Irma pressed her ear to his lips to hear him. "Give …a man …a moment."

Irma cast her eyes upward to where Bo stood, a dark figure against the sunny sky above him. She raised her palm, hoping he would interpret it properly as a sign to wait.

"Bjorn, I need to move you onto this mattress," she said into his ear.

There was a peculiar vibration in his chest before his mouth moved again. "Always …trying …to get me …"

A dry cough shook him before he continued. "Into bed, my …bride."

Irma could not hold back the laughter through her tears of relief.

After that, he roused enough to help her move his heavy form onto the mattress. The effort appeared to have exhausted him, however, and he looked as if he might lose consciousness again as she strapped him onto the pad that would, she hoped, lift him to safety.

Before signaling that they were ready to start the ascent up the cliff face, Irma leaned over Bjorn. "Hang on," she whispered into his ear, "and we will share a mattress soon enough, Bjorn of Adytum, my bridegroom."

As she raised her hand to signal Bo, Bjorn's eyes fluttered open again. "Irma." She detected urgency in his voice.

"Yes, my love?" Her hands ran compulsively over his form.

"Found …some …something," he gritted out. She followed the cast of his gaze downward to his fisted left hand.

His eyelashes fluttered against his tan skin. Irma opened his fist with gentle fingers and slipped them into his palm. Her eyes flashed back up to his, which were now closed. His hand slackened in her gentle grip.

To her astonishment, she raised to her eyes two golden circles. Both were intricately carved with the same decorative design, one was distinctly larger and thicker than the other.

They were …rings.

One for him.

One for her.

Slowly, as if testing it out, she slipped on the smaller one, finding that it fit her finger as if made for her.

Irma stared at him in shock. Perhaps he sensed her stare, for he said one more thing before they raised his body up.

"The island …provides."

****

Bjorn rose out of unconsciousness like a diver ascending from the ocean depths. He floated up only to be pulled down into the cold darkness again.

A sound urged him to continue upward, though, into ever lighter water. Upward, little by little, toward wakefulness.

Gradually, he became aware of two things.

First, his hands stung like they'd been pricked by a thousand needles. The stinging pain was most acute in his left hand. Was someone dabbing it with acid, by Thor's wrath?

Second, he was at the same time being quite thoroughly chewed out by a low female voice. Through a foggy haze he could make out the unflattering words here and there.

"…harebrained …arrogant …*vitskirtr* …foolish …idiot …*lodinkinni* …"

"*Lodinkinni*!" He tried to object, thinking that it was hardly fair to blame him for his shaggy hair. When the word came out a hoarse jumble, he tried to wet his dry lips and forced his eyes open.

For an instant, the feminine mutters ceased, as did the torturous cleaning of the wounds on his hands

"Bjorn!" His name was not a shout, but it was loud enough to make him wince, a reaction he knew was completely lost in the next moment when he felt a heavy, deliciously curved weight descend upon him. His next inbreath confirmed to him that his Mary Irmengard had pounced upon him, the warm mass of her hair bringing him her sweet fragrance, enhanced by the salt of the sea air.

Before he could open his eyes, she scattered tiny kisses on his cheeks and neck, the corner of his mouth. Her cool hand brushed his hair from his brow—perhaps it was a bit shaggy, the thought drifted through his hazed-over mind. Finally, sensing her expectant stare, he pried open his heavy eyelids and met the flash of her emerald gaze.

"Bjorn of Adytum, you foolish, wonderful, man," she murmured in low, worried tones, her eyes roaming over him in obvious relief.

"Sigyn, my queen…" Irma must have noticed the hoarseness of his voice because she pulled away from him and began manipulating some cushions at his back to raise up his head a few inches.

When he made to speak again, she put a finger to his lips and raised a wooden cup to his parched mouth. The cool water tasted like ambrosia. When he tipped the cup to drink deeply of it, she stilled him. "Not too much at once," she cautioned before allowing him to sip from it again.

Annoyed to be tended like a sick child, Bjorn tested out his voice again.

"Here now, my dear." He was pleased that his voice, though still rough, had some strength behind it. "Why am I being scolded thusly?"

"Yes, and well you deserve it," she said with renewed spirit. "Of all the idiotic, addlepated …"

Closing his eyes, Bjorn let the scold wash over him,

a smile on his lips. This was his warrior bride. He preferred this to the worried, coddling tone she'd used before.

He opened his eyes again, while Irma still took him to task for…what, exactly? He didn't fully understand just yet. He had tried to confront something on his own, without her? Something she thought he should have included her in? In this moment, all that mattered to him was that she was here with him and that he must be well enough for her to unleash her feminine anger on him.

While she talked, he took in the brightly lit, white-washed room, with its small window and narrow bed. The only blemish was a long, dirty smudge along the wall right beside the door, reminding Bjorn that he'd backed Irma against it the first time he'd been in here.

She had brought him back to her chamber, he realized. Satisfaction at that eased his mind even further. She wouldn't have done that if she'd been truly angry with him. A memory tickled his brain. When he had awoken, just now, she had called him Bjorn of Adytum. Aye, she was still his bride and he her groom.

Suddenly, he sat up. Irma's diatribe halted, and she looked at him, alert.

"What is it?" Irma sat back on her haunches, straddled above him on the bed.

"On the cliff." His memory returned in a dousing wave. "I found something …" He flexed his palms, looking into them. Covered in scrapes, fingernails torn, they bore the signs of damage. Not from a fight, he recalled, but from clinging to the rocks to save himself from falling.

"Aye." Lifting his gaze to hers, he saw her lips twist and couldn't decide if it was in a good way or a bad way.

Irma cradled his palm in hers and again applied a wet cloth to it that had him huffing out a pointed curse.

"You hurt yourself." That worried tone he did not like crept back into her voice.

"Ah, lass." He started to reassure her, but then a glint of gold caught his eye.

He grabbed at the hand wielding the cursed astringent-covered cloth and turned it over so that he could see—

"The ring," he murmured. "You found it!"

"*You* found it!" she said, exasperated. "And nearly killed yourself to get it!"

"Irma, no." He twined their fingers together, now senseless to any pain. "I saw the gold below me on the cliff, but I was returning to the cottage to get you when the cursed rock collapsed beneath my feet!"

She regarded him skeptically for a second before she appeared to accept what he had said. But then she challenged, "And why were you on the cliff path alone?"

"I'd heard someone approaching the cottage and went out to—" He broke off his explanation when he saw the tight look on her face.

"You went out alone because you were trying to protect me." Her voice was deceptively calm in a way he was wise enough to mistrust.

Bjorn reclined on the cushions behind him with a sigh. "That is true, Irma." He raised his gaze to hers again. "You will have to forgive me, for old habits die hard."

Turning her hand over in his again, he added hopefully, "I notice that you nonetheless wear the ring."

This time, he knew it was a smile that twisted the corner of that delicious mouth of hers. She lowered her lashes. "It fits perfectly."

Bjorn's hoarse laugh filled the small bedroom. "Of course, it does!" He smiled at her bent head. "But—wait." Memory struck him and he surveyed his own hands again. "Where is mine?"

Irma reached into a pocket on her tunic and held the other thick band out to him.

"You didn't put it on me?" He frowned at the thought.

He'd caught Irma off guard. "Well," she said, "you were unconscious, and—your hands! I would not have wanted to injure you just to put the ring on your finger."

Holding her gaze, Bjorn extended his hand, palm down.

Injure me. Just make me yours. He waited in expectation.

Irma wet her lips.

Though he had not said the words aloud, he knew she had understood him.

Without breaking eye contact, she gently clasped his wounded hand in hers. Expression serious, she eased the ring onto his finger, over the first knuckle and then the second, until the band lay at the base of his finger.

A wide smile broke over Bjorn's face. Irma returned the smile, and both of them laughed lightly.

Ah, that was what he had wanted.

Bjorn twined his hand again with hers, their rings clicking softly against each other at the contact. The strength of their union pulsed through their clasped hands, through the gold circles warming his finger and hers. In that moment, he knew they were as one for all eternity.

"You are right to scold me for leaving you as I did,

my dear." He aimed to be conciliatory even as he was compelled to explain himself. "But when I saw the rings half covered in dust on the slab of rock below me, I knew I wanted us to fetch them together. I was on my way to get you for that purpose when I fell. I am sorry to worry you." He leaned forward, brushed her lips with his.

"Worry me!" Irma scoffed but, even then, returned his kiss with a harder one of her own. "That is the least of it." She licked a tongue out to caress his lower lip. "However," she said consideringly, "as it happens, I suppose we did claim the rings together."

His thoughts scattering, he seized her in an open-mouthed kiss that very quickly raged into a sensual fire. Irma's hands were in his hair, tugging his head this way and that to shift the angle of their kiss. Bjorn's hands, now free, cupped her breasts, stroking his thumbs over the nipples he could feel hardening beneath her tunic. He groaned low into her mouth when, with a slight change of position, she ground her soft core against his stiffening shaft.

Irma ripped her mouth from his and stared at him from half-lidded eyes. "Well, now," she murmured. "That seems a sign of …healthy recovery." She rubbed herself against him again, gauging his reaction, and his eyes drifted closed in bliss. Seeking her lips again with his, he aimed to prove his fitness to complete his conjugal duty and thrust his cock against the leather-covered seam of her sex.

When he dropped his head to the wall behind him, he couldn't help his grunt as it hit a tender spot he hadn't been aware of, and Irma stilled above him.

"'S all right, lass." Squeezing her breasts in hands that no longer felt pain, he slit his eyes open again.

"Don't stop, goddess love you, don't stop."

Irma's emerald gaze scanned him carefully, her fingers moving to stroke over his temples, cheeks, beard, jaw, neck. A groan rumbled out from his chest.

"Perhaps …" Irma ran her tongue over her bottom lip. "Perhaps we just need to make you more *comfortable*." Gently, she wiggled him down until his head rested on the cushions behind him. He sighed in relief that she showed no signs of leaving him hard and aching for her.

As her hands began to work on extricating him from first his shirt and then her own, he said a prayer of thanks to the island goddess who had brought him here, who had reunited him with this magnificent woman.

"Don't fret," she soothed, having tossed their clothing over the side of the bed. His gaze lingered on the pale, pink-tipped orbs of those glorious breasts. Leaning forward on her knees, she balanced her weight above him. "I'll be very careful with you."

And she was.

Bjorn knew he was a lucky man. He would not do anything to jeopardize her.

Yet there were still things left unspoken between them, things that threatened their newfound happiness.

Chapter 14

Some while later, after she had ridden him to a stunning climax, the blazing heat of passion faded into a warm contentment in his chest. He certainly suffered no pain.

Though it was true he had not lasted long this time, he blamed the intensity of their need, the urgency of her sexual demand. They had come together like a sudden storm, rising, peaking, and then fading into a quiet aftermath.

Despite his prone position, as she had bounced above him in a mad gallop, he'd slid his finger between them along her bud until her cries of pleasure had echoed off the walls. Only then had he given in to his own release.

Now Irma lay curled into his body, his arm around her, their breaths rising and falling in synchrony, the lingering moisture of their sweat and passion cooling on their bodies. Bjorn looked down at the river of her red hair streaming over his body. His mouth curved in lazy satisfaction.

Irma idly trailed one finger down the center of his chest, down the line of hair that led to his groin. But after a moment, her finger stilled.

"Bjorn …"

With the arm that cuddled her to his chest, he pressed her closer. "Anything, my dear." His voice was husky with the remnants of their passion, his lips against her hair.

"When we make love," she said, her tone curious, "you withdraw at the end."

Bjorn's feeling of warm contentment suddenly grew cold. When he realized he'd stopped breathing, he forced himself to draw in air steadily again and release it just as smoothly. Nevertheless, he knew that she had noticed his reaction. She lifted up to look at him, her arms a soft weight on his chest.

"Since we are well and truly wed …" A small smile played around her lips. "There is no need for that. We would make brawny babes with quick wits, don't you think?"

He knew what she wanted from him. Knew what reaction she would expect. But he could not give it. His face became a stony mask, words stuck in his throat.

That teasing smile disappeared, a small furrow forming between her brows. "There's a reason." It wasn't a question.

He wound his fingers into her hair, combed the strands back from her brow.

As the silence wore on, he wondered if he could just …never answer her. Perhaps a well-aimed joke to distract her? He found there was no humor within him.

Bjorn's eyes met hers again, and he knew he had to tell her.

He heaved a heavy sigh and closed his eyes. Irma's weight settled atop him as she waited for him to find the words.

"My …first wife," he said. Irma tensed, and he tightened his arm around her. "Her name was Dagmar. She was—" He had to swallow before continuing. "She was a beautiful woman, sweet, delicate."

When Irma's hand lifted to stroke his beard, he knew she had already guessed his worst, his last, his guiltiest secret. He forced himself to continue.

"We were married for many months before she conceived but, when it came time for the child to be born—" Bjorn broke off as the old emotion choked him, preventing him from continuing.

"Did she die in childbed?" Irma posed the question as gently as she could.

He could only nod.

"And the babe?"

He shook his head once, heard her small sound of sympathetic distress.

"It was …it was a bad business," he admitted when he had found his voice again.

"You were there?"

"At the end." His expression was strained with tension. "I could not bear to hear her suffering. I tried to help her." He flexed his hands, remembering them stained with blood.

"Bjorn, I am so sorry," Irma murmured.

After a long moment where he witnessed behind closed lids the terrible scene of Dagmar's passing—her eyes accusing, the life draining from them—he felt Irma shift above him. She tucked one arm into his side, settled the other over his stomach. Then she pressed her face to his chest, kissed him lightly there, gifted him with the living warmth of her body.

It allowed him to continue. "She and I," he said, "we did not share a great love, but she was a good woman. I know she blamed me, at the end. I blamed myself." He followed with the words that had looped in his mind since that catastrophic day. "She deserved better. I should have protected her."

Instead of feeling a release at the admission, the heavy burden of his guilt burned in his gut. He had vowed once never to claim another woman as his own and had broken that vow for Irma. But he could not break his other promise. He would not risk the woman he loved in such a way. He could not.

Long moments passed, not so contentedly as before. Bjorn could practically hear the whir of Irma's thoughts.

At last she voiced the question on her mind. "You do not want a child?"

"Children are a blessing." His reply came without hesitation.

"Then you do not want a child *with me*?"

At that, he struggled upright. "I will not risk you." He captured her upper arms in his hands so that she could see the conviction in his eyes. "I must, *I will* keep you safe."

When Irma stiffened in his arms, her lips thinning stubbornly, he knew he had said the wrong thing.

"*Safe.*" She spat the word like it was a curse on her tongue.

She ripped herself from his grasp so fast he dropped back onto the cushions behind him. As the cool of the room chilled his skin in her absence, he watched her dressing with vigorous intent, covering all that lovely voluptuousness as if donning battle gear.

Only when she was fully armored did she turn back to him, her expression set.

"What happened to her, to your Dagmar, was a great tragedy. I am sorry, so very sorry, for her pain, and yours. But," she added, placing her hands on her hips, "I do not need a man to keep me *safe*. I never have."

"Irma—"

"No." With one hand she made a sharp, cutting motion. "Life is risk. You should know that. I learned the costs of battle by your side. *Men*." She rolled her eyes. "You think that waging war only happens among you. But every woman who gives birth wages a battle, a noble one. The battle for new life. There are no guarantees, not even here. But I will not live a half-life under a man's 'protection.'"

"You cannot—"

"I am strong enough in myself," she said overtop his protest. "When you understand what that means, Bjorn of Adytum, you will understand the woman you have taken to wife." She paused, hand on the door, and looked over her shoulder. "Then you can find me."

With that, she stepped out of the room. The door closed with a soft click behind her, but he heard it like the sharpest crack of thunder.

Bjorn dragged his scratched-up hands across his eyes and allowed the weight of grief, old and new now combined, to engulf him in sorrow.

****

At some point, sleep overwhelmed his misery and the throb of a renewed headache. When next he woke, it was to a knock at the door.

"Oy! Bjorn!" said a male voice he recognized.

Bjorn winced. Misery and headache still raging in tandem, he noted.

Despite his lack of answer, the jingle of the door latch preceded Bo's entry into the room. The younger man came in with his characteristic nimble energy, bearing a tray with a variety of vessels on it, one of which smelled of some kind of tea.

Bjorn wrinkled his nose. "Not hungry." He sounded like a petulant child, but he could not bring himself to care.

"Having a good sulk, then?" Bo nodded as if this was exactly as he'd expected. Drier now than the last time Bjorn had seen him, spiky hair standing up on his crown as usual, Bo set the tray on top of Irma's dressing cabinet. "Mum always said the best cure for that was—" He whisked a small wooden plate under Bjorn's nose with a flourish. "—blackberry tart!"

Bjorn looked at Bo from under heavy brows, unimpressed. Bo didn't notice. He had turned back to the tray, busying himself with its contents, and when he turned around again, he held the small tart-bearing plate and a cup filled with some steaming beverage, one in each hand.

Bo handed Bjorn the beverage. "Angelina says to drink this first. Doesn't smell good, but it's best to do as Angelina says."

Bjorn reflexively accepted the cup but gazed into it suspiciously.

"It's for your head." Bo rapped his knuckles against the shaved side of his own scalp.

Medicine, Bjorn realized. He wasn't so foolish as to say no to that. Sipping at it cautiously, he decided it wasn't too bad. Bitter, yes, and yet there was also some fresh herbaceous flavor that made it drinkable.

"And now that you've had some of that," Bo said, once Bjorn had drunk about half the cup. "You can have the tart."

His first impulse was to sullenly declare he had no appetite. When his stomach rumbled, however, Bjorn reluctantly accepted the pastry. After one small bite—*by the goddess that was delicious*—he wolfed down the rest of it in two gulps.

Thinking of the last time he'd seen Bo, during the scuffle in the meadow, and his own subsequent conversation with Andor, Bjorn asked a question at the forefront of his mind.

"What's become of Harald?" He decided to get straight to the most important point. "Andor told me he was half crazed and not to be trusted with the women." It was frustrating that he was not yet strong enough of body and spirit to see this for himself.

"As to that …" Bo drew the words out. "Andor may be right. We had Harald contained."

"Good," pronounced Bjorn.

"But he, er, he managed to escape."

Bjorn issued a string of curses. "What has he done?" He uttered his words through gritted teeth.

Bo leaned back against the wall, looking pensive. "Not sure," he said finally. "We don't know where he is."

"And Astrid? How does she fare?"

"Astrid?" Bo shot him a narrow-eyed look.

"For the love of the goddess, Bo, Astrid must be here."

The other man merely shrugged. "If she is," he said, "the nuns have her well-guarded, I suspect." Noticing that Bo did not make eye contact when he said the words, Bjorn wondered what lay behind them.

Bo directed Bjorn to drink the rest of the tea, which Bjorn had to admit had settled his brains somewhat. The ebbing of pain brought physical relief but no comfort to his ravaged spirit.

The younger man refilled Bjorn's cup from a small earthen pot on the tray and brought forth …another tart. "Angelina judged you would need a larger dose of tea and a larger repast than more sensibly sized fellows like me."

"True enough, *Minimus.*" Bjorn smirked when Bo pretended offense at the appellation. "So I have Angelina to thank."

He had to admit, Bo's mum had been very wise. Bjorn's spirits were lifting at the ingestion of the piquantly sweet berries wrapped in a flaky pastry.

"It's a very good tart," he added around a mouthful of the confection. Despite his intentions, he failed to eat the second tart more slowly. "Please extend my thanks to your woman."

"Oh, Angelina made the tea. She has a way with herbs and restoratives. The tart is Sister Benita's. Her cooking even gives Mum's competition." Bo's gaze grew thoughtful.

Bjorn recalled the island's chef with whom he had spoken in the dining hall, the one who had made the delicious meat pie but who, more importantly, had given him Irma's name. He sat back on his cushions with a groan.

"I thank them—and you—for thinking of me." Bjorn heaved a deep, miserable sigh. "Bo, I've cocked it up."

"Aye," Bo agreed and then straightened with an innocent look at Bjorn's scowl. "You said it, not me." Handing Bjorn a third tart and refilling his cup again, Bo added, "But it wasn't me or Angelina or Benita who's responsible for this." He gestured with the pot.

With a start of hope, Bjorn met the other man's eyes

directly. "Do you mean—? Was it Irma who—"

"Of course it was Irma! Very worried about you, she is." Bo turned his back to fiddle with the tray again.

"Well, she could be worrying about me *here*," Bjorn grumbled.

"Not if you cocked it up, brother. That's not a female's way." This last the younger man said sagely.

"Bo," he said, making the decision to confide in him despite his slightly annoying overconfidence in this area. "I lost one wife to childbed. You do not know what that was like." The memory of that terrible day burned in his gut. "I cannot lose another, and not this one. I must keep her …" He struggled against using the word "safe" that Irma so evidently despised. Instead, he concluded, "I must protect her from that most womanly danger if I can."

Bo pressed his lips together as if Bjorn had said something deeply stupid.

"I know she is strong." Bjorn defended himself in the ensuing silence. "She is brave and fierce and sharp-witted. But I will not sacrifice her, nor let her sacrifice herself."

After a long moment, Bo sat down at the foot of the narrow bed. The question he asked surprised Bjorn.

"How do you think you got here?"

Bjorn frowned at him in confusion. "Here?"

Bo cast his eyes around the bedchamber. "Here. Or even, off the cliffs. How do you think you *got here*, man?"

Bjorn felt like the veriest idiot, but he did not know what Bo was getting at.

"I don't know," he said finally. "I suppose someone found me—"

"Who found you?" Bo raised his eyebrows.

"Did—Was it Irma?"

"Of course it was." Bo raised his hands in exasperation. "She tracked you from your little cottage to the cliffs and deduced what had happened. Otherwise we might never have found you. And then what do you think happened?"

"She, well, she must have gotten help."

"Aye, that she did," confirmed his friend. "Me and Njal and Angelina and half the other people on this island. You're not a lean and sensibly proportioned man like me." He patted his abdomen and flashed his white teeth. "So there was much to do. She oversaw the whole operation, put together a fecking pulley machine to hoist you up."

Warm admiration filled Bjorn. "That's my lass. I said she was sharp-witted, did I not?"

"She was as cool and resourceful as the most seasoned general," Bo continued. "You should have seen everyone hopping to do her will as she snapped out orders. Me included!" Bo laughed and shook his head.

Yes, Bjorn could see it in his mind's eye.

"And when we were ready to send the contraption down to bring you back up, Bjorn," Bo's tone grew more serious, "who do you think rappelled down the cliff to you? Who put you on the pad and tied you in so you would not fall again? Who sent you up and then climbed back up again with nothing but a length of rope and grim determination?"

Bjorn's jaw dropped.

"She went down the cliff face? But—" His mind's eye again supplied an image, this time of the jagged, uneven, and crumbling edge of the sea cliffs. Bone-deep fear and a surge of hot fury swept from his core up his neck. "You let her—with the danger that she might—how could you—?"

Bo lifted his hands again. "She did it herself, man, she did it herself. It was her choice and, more than that," he added, pointing sternly at Bjorn, "it was the right choice. She knows those cliffs. She's strong and agile, and she wasn't too heavy to be lifted up if something went wrong."

"But she could have—" This time Bjorn's mind went blank at the thought of Irma tumbling down the cliffs as she tried to rescue him.

"She also protected herself," Bo interrupted. "She had a …a harness type of thing she wore. Ingenious really. These nuns! They've thought of everything!" He flashed another grin at Bjorn and shrugged. "It would have caught her had she lost her grip at any point. But she didn't."

Bjorn lay silent, thinking about all Bo had said. Irma had risked her very life for his. And she had done it not recklessly or arrogantly but with great strategy and care. He owed her his life. More than that, he realized, he owed her his deepest respect.

"Ah, the goddess." He moaned, tilting his head to the ceiling. "*I have cocked this up*."

"That you have," agreed Bo. "Are you going to fix it?"

"Will she even let me?" he grumbled.

Bo shrugged. "Never knew you to give up the field, Bjorn."

Once Bo had left, taking the empty tray with him, Bjorn laid his head back and closed his eyes.

Did he dare risk losing her? He remembered what

she had said, *Life is risk.*

And wasn't that the truth of it?

It was evident that bearing a child was a risk she wanted to take, or at least, wanted to be able to choose should she wish it.

Images chased through his mind.

One of Irma, belly round with their child.

Another of Irma cradling an infant in her arms.

Yet another, of him this time, a red-haired moppet on his shoulders.

This last hit him like a punch to his gut.

It would be good. It would be a dream.

It would be …worth the risk.

Feeling the earth shift under him, his long-ago vow crumbling like the cliff had done by the sea path, Bjorn knew that he would have to trust Irma with this. He would trust himself and her together. Whatever the future held for them.

What he did not know was whether she would forgive him for being a right idiot.

On his next breath, more of her words came to him.

I am strong enough in myself. When you understand what that means, Bjorn of Adytum, you will understand the woman you have taken to wife. Then you can find me.

Even angry, even as she had left, she had called him Bjorn of Adytum, he realized with a modicum of satisfaction. She had acknowledged herself as his wife.

All right then. He believed he understood. Now he must find her. Then he would prove it to her.

Chapter 15

"We are in agreement?" Mother Agnes asked the small group gathered in her solarium.

A murmur of voices assented, but the sound was not exactly enthusiastic.

Rays of afternoon sunshine streamed through the windows of the room that sat at the top of the Abbey, lighting up faces here and there while it cast others in shadow.

Sister Mary Irmengard kept her silence.

"Very well." Agnes seemed pleased at the apparent consensus. "Angelina, we need you to get Sister Frances from the sick ward. As the musical director of the *ceolchoirm*, she will need to prepare the new arrangements we will use for the equinox ritual."

"Yes, Mother." Angelina gave the woman who was both the Mother Superior and her own mother a wide-eyed look and dashed through the solarium doorway.

At any other time, Mother Agnes would have found that look suspicious, but she had already turned away, hastening along the impromptu meeting at which they were now gathered. "The rest of you, please attend to your part of the ceremony with diligence. May we return the Abbey to the refuge it has been these last twenty years. You are dismissed."

The gathered women began to move out, some alone, others in small groups.

Perhaps Mother Agnes had not been oblivious to Angelina's dubious agreement after all, for she followed out of the solarium closely on Angelina's heels.

Glancing around at them, Irma wondered what the other women here were thinking.

She breathed through a pervading sense of unease. She did not like being at odds with any of the other women of Adytum, but especially not Mother Agnes, for whom she had profound respect. Irma knew very well that they had Agnes to thank for how efficiently and harmoniously the Abbey ran. Agnes's compassionate authority was the stable foundation for everything they did and were—for two decades.

And in the time since Irma had last seen Bjorn, Mother Agnes had developed a plan to expel the men from the island.

Irma didn't like it.

At all.

Mainly because, she admitted, she did not want the men to leave. One man in particular would certainly not be leaving, not if Irma had anything to say about it. Somewhat to her surprise, Irma found she'd come to like the other men as well—for the most part. At any rate, she thought she could work with them, should they remain. Which she hoped they would. Surprisingly.

Irma also didn't like that Mother Agnes's plan did not involve a direct challenge or even a negotiation, her own preferred modes of problem-solving. Rather, Agnes's plan invoked the will of the goddess, called forth through the powerful, communal equinox ritual, the *ceolchoirm*.

The nuns at the Abbey performed the formal service at the spring equinox each year. It was a celebration of the new season, of lengthening days and new life. Irma quite enjoyed the ritual, especially since Frances had arrived and brought an array of musical talents to the annual event.

Mother Agnes, along with the other nuns gathered in her solarium this afternoon, intended to use this celebration to call upon their divine protector to drive the men off the island.

With all that Irma had experienced since the men had arrived, this intention seemed—well, it seemed contrary to the will of the goddess, if she had to name it. The goddess had, it appeared, called the men to the island, allowed them entry despite their strong defenses, prevented blood from flowing among them …perhaps even left rings with which to tie at least one nun to one barbarian in union.

A union that Irma hoped, one day, might itself bring forth new life. If Bjorn could accept the dangers that came with it, that is. Irma gazed down at the gold band that even now graced her finger, touching it with her thumb.

This plan of Mother Agnes's felt wrong, in her gut.

It was strange to be on the other side of Mother Agnes. They two had worked together compatibly for fifteen years, and Irma had great respect for the other woman's rational and empathetic leadership. Some intense emotion was driving Mother Agnes, though. Irma had never seen the other woman in such a state. The abbess was determined, single-mindedly so, to expel the men from the island. And there were enough other women who seemed to share that determination that this plan had come to fruition.

Agnes claimed that she was protecting Astrid, but

Irma thought there was more Agnes was not saying. Based on what Irma had seen, protecting Astrid only required containing Harald—not that they had yet managed to do that satisfactorily. Given what she knew of her groom, Irma did not think Bjorn would be party to anything that put Astrid, or any other woman, in danger.

Yet, it was true also that this plan did not require much of anything from Irma except her compliance. This was, after all, not the direct and physical way Irma fought. Irma was simply one among many who would lend their voices to invoke the goddess.

Could she participate even though it went against what she knew to be wise? Even though it went against what she wanted in her heart of hearts? Perhaps she should simply leave it to the goddess's will to respond or not.

Irma shook her head and exhaled with a soft, "Bah!"

Most of the other women, Irma noticed, had dispersed to continue their preparations for the *ceolchoirm*. Eager to leave the solarium and Mother Agnes behind, Irma started toward the door.

"Sister Mary Irmengard?"

Startled at the high-pitched, slightly husky voice coming so quickly on the heels of her somewhat disloyal thoughts, Irma turned to see Sister Grace at her elbow. When Irma paused, Grace gave her head a small shake and urged Irma out of the solarium to the sunlit terrace that ringed the Abbey's top tier.

"Yes, Sister Grace?" she said curiously once they were in the open air.

"Perhaps, you would—" Grace cast a quick glance at the solarium behind them. "Might I speak with you a moment?" Her voice was only a bit above a whisper.

Irma bent down to the little nun. "In private?" Sensing Grace's nervousness, Irma gentled her tone. Grace merely nodded and darted ahead of her, tripping lightly down the stone staircase that led to the main hall. Partway down, though, she made a quick move to the right, and Irma followed her into a narrow passageway leading to a storage room that connected to the Library in the Abbey's westward wing.

Once Grace had opened the heavy wooden door and ushered Irma into the chamber, she stood with her back against the closed door, nervously twining her fingers together.

"You wanted to speak, Sister Grace?" Irma tried to keep her voice low and encouraging. Though Grace was a fully grown adult, there was a perpetually young and innocent quality about her that brought out Irma's protective tendencies. She also did her best not to let her size and strength intimidate the other woman. In that spirit, Irma sat herself on a large wooden trunk in the middle of the room.

Aiming for patience while she waited for Grace to speak, she watched the dust motes drift in the rectangular beam of sunlight coming from a slitted window.

She finally interrupted the ensuing silence, hoping she didn't sound as impatient as she was in truth. "Is it about the *ceolchoirm*?"

Grace's eyes flashed to hers. "Yes," she whispered. She straightened her back against the door and continued. "I have seen you with your bear."

Irma crossed her arms and settled on the trunk. This was a curious turn of conversation. Irma remembered that Grace had been with them on the cliff path for the rescue. "Bjorn, yes. What of him?"

"He seems, well, he seems very nice." Grace peered at Irma from beneath her lashes.

Irma could not help her puzzled look.

"He is." Though "nice" was not a word she would have used. Bjorn was strong and bold, trustworthy and honorable, fiercely attractive and passionate, joyful—and fun.

He had brought laughter back into her life when she hadn't known she'd been missing it.

Not that she had seen him since their argument in her bedchamber. She told herself she was leaving him to heal in peace—and giving him time to come to his senses about the woman he had so recently wed. If he didn't soon come to her, Irma knew, she would go to him. She was not one to avoid a problem. And they would resolve it, one way or another.

"More than that." She looked steadily at Grace. "He is my love."

Grace nodded. Her eyes scanned Irma's face and saw the truth of Irma's raw statement. "It's only that …" Grace looked to the side, then met Irma's resolute gaze once more. "Don't you want him to stay?" she asked in a rapid burst.

Now wasn't this interesting? "Do you have a man you'd like to stay as well, Grace?" Irma asked instead of answering.

Grace's lips firmed mulishly. "I asked you. Do you want the men expelled from the island as Mother Agnes intends? Including your man?"

Irma experienced a flash of admiration for little Grace's show of spirit. It compelled an honest response.

After a long moment, Irma conceded, "No. No, I do not want them expelled." She finally said aloud what she had been thinking privately. "I think they should stay."

A bright smile transforming her visage, Grace clapped her hands together. "I told them you would!" The younger woman skipped over to where Irma sat on the trunk and perched lightly beside her.

"There's a group of us," Grace whispered conspiratorially even though they were the only ones in the clutter-filled chamber. "Do you remember, in the Library, before? When we all met and Alice was saying that there was nothing in the Sacred Scripts to force the men to leave?"

Irma did remember, as she remembered the undercurrents between Grace and Sister Alice about what wisdom the ancient texts contained.

"Didn't Mother Agnes just tell us all that Alice had indeed found the words we needed to say within the *ceolchoirm*?"

Grace waved her off. "Well, as to that—" But she halted when the door creaked open.

Sister Alice's face peeked through the crack in the door for an instant before she pushed her way in.

"There you are!" Alice said. "What does Irma think?"

Irma flicked her gaze back and forth between the two women.

"I was just telling her"—Grace's gaze flickered back to Irma—"that you have found a special set of words for the *ceolchoirm*."

"Yes, Irma, I did." Sister Alice's tone was gravely serious.

"Words that would…expel the men?" asked Irma, feeling she had gotten herself in the middle of a prior conversation.

Sister Alice shot Sister Grace a frustrated glance. "I thought you told her!"

"I was just getting to it!"

"She thinks we're still planning to get rid of the men."

"But I was right that she *doesn't want* them to leave. She wants her bear."

"Bjorn," Irma corrected, irritated to be talked about as if she were not present.

"I had to make sure," Grace added to Alice.

"So you did not find a way to remove the men from Adytum?" Irma asked.

"Oh, no," Grace confirmed. "Alice says there are no words to expel the men. It's just the opposite."

"The …opposite?" Irma repeated with a frown. "You want to bring more men to the island?"

"No!" Grace and Alice said at the same time.

"We want *our men* to stay," Alice continued. "As you want yours to stay."

"But Mother Agnes thinks the ritual will make them all leave."

Alice and Grace exchanged a guilty look.

"Yes, you see, that's because it's what I told her." Alice blushed at the admission.

Irma raised her eyebrows. To lie deliberately to the abbess! Irma would never have thought such a thing possible, especially from these two sisters.

At her look of surprise and—truthfully—disapproval, Grace and Alice began talking at once until Alice placed a gentle hand over Grace's mouth to silence her.

"Let me, Grace," Alice said. "Sister Irma, I think you agree with us that the men should stay with us. If they want, that is. Is that correct?"

Having already admitted as much to Grace, Irma agreed readily. "Yes, that's correct."

"As I've said many times," Alice continued, her exasperation evident, "it is not clear that anyone can simply leave Adytum once they have arrived here. When I was reading the texts, it is true that I saw no clues as to how we might eject the men who have arrived here. Unless we were to use violent means." She gestured to Irma as if acknowledging this as Irma's preferred method.

Irma lifted her hands. "I did try that way."

"Exactly. In fact, their immunity to violence and ability to get through our many defenses suggests that they are part of the—" She broke off, looking uncertainly at Irma.

"Go on," Irma said impatiently.

"Well, I know you are of a practical nature, but the texts—"

"Yes, Sister Alice," Irma interrupted. "You may be sure that I am aware there is some force beyond us pulling strings since the men arrived."

"Sister Catherine says even before," Grace chimed in only to fall silent again after a quelling look from Alice.

"Sister Catherine?" Irma's voice was sharp. "Has the goddess communicated through the Oracle about the matter?"

The two women merely looked at each other.

"Sister Catherine is one of us," Alice revealed finally. "She also wants the men to stay, and more than that, she believes, as we do, that it is part of a forewarned destiny I discovered in the Sacred Scripts."

Destiny. Irma thought of how Bjorn had returned to her life. *Yes, it does have the feel of that.*

"We must bring about our own destiny," Irma replied after a moment, thinking of the rings Bjorn had found among the island's rocky escarpment and what both of them had risked to attain them.

Grace swung her head toward Alice. "See, I told you she would understand."

"Understand! You've told me almost nothing!" Irma declared in frustration.

"We must bring about the destiny foreshadowed. It is up to us. And so, though we *suggested* to Mother Agnes that we had found a way to eject the men, we found instead something …else."

Irma considered this carefully vague statement. "You found a way to turn the equinox ritual into a call for the men to stay."

"In a way," Alice hedged. "But first—" she leveled a serious look at Irma, "—are you with us?"

Irma just shook her head at this. "You know that I am." Irma was aware that her affections would be obvious to anyone who had witnessed what had happened on the cliffs. "Or we would not be having this conversation."

Her two sisters smiled, and Alice said, "Let me tell you what we've found."

And then she did.

****

Bjorn knew he was moping.

Actually, what he was trying to do was to find Irma so that he could throw himself at her feet and beg forgiveness.

He also could not help the fear that lingered.

Exposing Irma to the dangers of childbirth seemed like stepping off a cliff face and hoping to be held aloft.

Again, he supposed.

And so he'd trailed her around the convent and the grounds since he had the strength to rise from her bed. But, he admitted to himself, nerves and fear had dampened his drive to catch up to her.

"Last I saw, she was headed to the dairy," Sister Benita of the magnificent pastries told him, no little irritation in her tone. She pointed to a side door that led out of the kitchens and turned back to the carrots she was hacking with a large, very sharp knife.

"You display excellent knife skills." Perhaps flattery would soften her. But she merely rolled her eyes. "You've the makings of a fine swordsman, I think," he added, mostly to distract her while he nipped two carrot chunks from the pile on the block before her. "Swordswoman."

"Hey!" she shouted at his retreating back. Chuckling around his crunchy snack, he heard her mutter, "*Knife skills*, he says …"

The kitchen's side door opened out onto a courtyard. Bjorn followed the sounds of mooing to a barn and a large open shed. No flash of red caught his eye, but another sound came to his ears and gave him a jolt.

It was the cry of a baby.

Bjorn froze in place.

A baby, here? He shook his head. He was almost ready to turn back toward the Abbey when a curly haired woman came into view. Sitting upright in her arms was a squalling bundle of humanity.

"Now what's the trouble?" she was saying to the babe conversationally. "I've been walking with you for the last half of an hour. You've had your dinner, and it's time for—"

The woman saw Bjorn standing in the courtyard and stopped.

Surprised by this, the baby also ceased its cries, turning its tear-streaked cheeks to Bjorn.

He saw the little lip poke out, the miniature face crumple, and he was certain the babe would start bawling again. But instead, it reached out a little arm and pointed a tiny, imperative finger at him. "Da!"

Bjorn looked to the woman and saw a smile crease her pretty countenance.

"Da! Da!" The child looked at the woman, its intention clear. The little finger pointed again. "Da!"

Amusement colored her voice. "He wants to meet you." The woman's brown eyes sparkled.

Bjorn cautiously stepped forward. When he offered his hand, instead of taking it, the child launched himself bodily at Bjorn, and he found himself with an armful of blanketed babe. The boy's grin displayed two teeth on his lower gums and no more, and Bjorn had to laugh.

"Hail to you, fine sir," Bjorn said as the baby chortled merrily in delighted response. He bounced the child lightly in his arms.

The woman before him stretched her arms to the sky, then shook them out. "Thanks for that. He's a weight on the arms, he is, but as cuddly a boy as a mama could wish."

"He's yours?" Bjorn asked, though it was obvious as the child shared the mother's curly black hair and big brown eyes.

"That he is." Pride rang through her voice. "I'm Sister Colleen," she added. "I tend the dairy."

"Did you—?" He paused, knowing his question was nosy.

"Go on, then." She folded her arms over her ample chest.

"Did you bring him here with you?"

"In a way." The dimple reappeared in her cheek before she turned and began tidying up a variety of pails strewn about the yard. After a minute she turned back to him. "I arrived here shortly before he was born."

Little baby fingers tugged on Bjorn's ear, and Bjorn gave the babe his own fingers to play with instead. "You had the child here? On the island?"

"That I did." She looked at him with curiosity. "That surprises you?"

"Nothing about this island should surprise me by now." He shook his head as the baby began twisting the gold band around the base of his finger. "But—yes, yes, it does surprise me. This is a convent, and you are all …nuns." It seemed ridiculous to point out the obvious.

The curly-haired woman looked back at him with quiet seriousness. "The women of Adytum may be nuns, but they are not ignorant of the world and its workings." Her gaze was caught by a large cow wandering toward them, and she walked over to it, stroking its head when it gave a low moo.

"I arrived here about a year ago, definitely *not* a nun"—she cast him a rueful glance—"and frightened out of my wits, as you might imagine." Sister Colleen fiddled distractedly with the cow's ear, which twitched in response.

"Mmoo!" said the baby boy, pointing this time at the cow. Bjorn walked him toward his mother and the animal under her gentle hand.

"Bredon was just about ready to make his entry into the world. Weren't you, my boy?" she said, her gaze soft on the child leaning down to gently pat the cow's neck. "The women here …" Colleen shook her head. "They were so kind, so competent. My boat had moored on the rocks, and I was in no state to hoist myself out. But Sister Mary Irmengard—"

"Irma!"

"Oh, if you know her, then you know I had nothing to fear after that."

"Did she—" Bjorn stuttered to a halt as blood-streaked images assailed him.

"At the birth, she attended me, along with Sister Angelina, Sister Catherine, and Mother Agnes, of course." The woman's big brown eyes grew distant with memory.

"And you were—it was—" Bjorn swallowed heavily. He did not know how to put his question into words, but the woman seemed to understand.

Brown eyes turning sharp again, she said, "It was difficult, yes, but so …beautiful. And I have my little Bredon as reward."

"And Irma, she—"

Sister Colleen laughed lightly. "You know Irma. So strong and practical! She directed everything with so little effort I didn't even realize it at the time. And I had her voice in my ear the whole way through, telling me to be brave, that I was the fiercest of warriors bringing in new life, telling me how glorious it would be at the end. And she was right." A bright smile lit the woman's face, and she reached up to trace a finger over her baby's pink cheek.

At that, the boy sat upright again in Bjorn's arms and

patted his shoulder. He chattered unintelligibly to Bjorn, his large brown eyes serious and strangely wise.

"Yes, fine sir, I take your meaning," Bjorn replied with equal solemnity.

"Sister Irma ..." Colleen's voice was gentle. "She can seem so invulnerable. But for all her strength, she has a woman's soft heart."

Bjorn knew it was true, knew he had to honor all of her many facets. His feet were steadier on the ground beneath him.

When the boy's little fists came up to rub his eyes, his mother lifted her hands for him. Bjorn passed him over with, to his surprise, no little reluctance.

He could have one of these for his own, he realized with wonder.

"And now it's time for our nap," Colleen said, and the babe laid its head sweetly on her shoulder. "Fare-thee-well," she called to Bjorn over her shoulder. "Good luck with Irma. I hope you are worthy of her." Another flash of her dimple and the woman strolled away from him and toward the barn.

Bjorn looked to his remaining companion. "I will be." He fisted the hand that bore his marital ring. "I will be worthy of her."

As he turned his back to reenter the convent, truly intent on finding Irma now, his companion answered him with a long, low moo.

Bjorn's laugh echoed through the small yard.

Chapter 16

Later in the evening, Irma entered the main hall and stalked over to the table on which she'd set up her chess match. As she'd expected, the black pieces had advanced upon her. She had been playing against her unseen adversary all day, and she was frustrated to find herself well matched. Not yet outmatched, though.

But, as she stood surveying the field of play, hands on her hips, she was surprised at what she saw.

Someone else had moved a white piece. It was, she had to admit, a good move.

Just as she reached out to touch the piece that had shifted position, a large arm suddenly wrapped around her waist from behind.

Reflexively, she shot her elbow into the hard abdomen behind her—eliciting a satisfying grunt—and lifted her foot to stomp on his instep. But she was thwarted when the man behind her lifted her bodily, both of her feet dangling in the air, and tilted her at an angle until her body rested fully against his.

"Settle down, lass, it's only me," murmured a voice she recognized. Bjorn's warm breath tickled the shell of her ear, raising the hairs along her nape and arms.

"Feeling better, I see." Irma's reply was as sharp as her elbow. The unsteadiness of her voice irritated her, but she blamed it on the meaty arm holding her aloft across her midsection. Irma hooked her legs around his thighs to take some of her weight off his arm.

He nuzzled the side of her face in response, interpreting her move correctly as an indication that her anger at him was fading.

"In body, yes," he whispered against her cheek, "but I am still wounded in heart and spirit." He rested his bearded chin against her temple. "What must I do to earn your forgiveness?"

It was strange, having this conversation with him without being able to see his expression. Irma reached up a hand to the back of his skull, carefully avoiding his head wound. She tipped her head until her mouth was a hair's breadth away from his. "Set me down, Bjorn of Adytum, so we may speak as equals."

Straightening and then bending forward slightly, Bjorn let her feet touch the ground though his arm remained a hard band around her waist. "I fear what I will see on your face," he admitted softly, "should I let you go."

Irma let herself go limp for a second, fooling him into thinking she would let him have his way. Then she suddenly twisted herself under his arm so that their chests pressed tightly together, bosom to bosom and eye to eye. Emerald green met the green of the forest floor as their gazes met, searched.

Though she could see he was much improved, Irma observed the remnants of pain and grief in the lines on his tanned face.

"Do you know me?" she asked finally, aware he would understand the question.

"Aye, that I do, Irma." Bjorn cupped her shoulders in his wide palms, bending toward her so that she could not mistake his meaning. "I thought I did earlier when I recognized you as Signus and Yrse from those many years ago. But now I see the woman you have become. Bo told me how you pulled me from the cliffs."

She opened her lips to speak, and he pressed a finger to them. "When the stark terror of what might have happened to you there diminished," he continued with a wry twist of his mouth, "I realized that I was …not at all surprised at what you had done and how bravely and competently you had done it. In fact, it seemed the most likely thing of all."

This time when she made to respond, he simply talked over her. "You are a beautiful, voluptuous creature, my dear." Bjorn said the words over her protest, his palms swiping downward to skim her waist and hips and back up again. "And you possess a fierce capacity to love. But that is not all you are. You are a warrior in truth, a warrior among women, a warrior among warriors." He rested his forehead against hers, using those stroking hands to ease her into the cradle of his body. "I will never doubt you again, and I will not withhold any part of myself from you," he murmured into her ear. "You are my queen, my Sigyn, and I am your humble knight. I shall fight alongside you but never in place of you."

Irma breathed in the salty masculine scent at the base of his neck and exhaled it in a relieved sigh. "You no longer fear what might happen in childbirth?" She had to be sure.

He pulled back quickly. "I did not say that. I do fear it." Irma saw the desperation of it in his eyes, but before she could respond he continued. "More than I fear the loss of my own life, I fear the loss of yours."

Irma acknowledged his statement in sympathetic

silence. Having witnessed him splayed along the rocks, she understood him well. Her hand stroked his chest, aiming to soothe his rapidly beating heart.

"Today I met your Sister Colleen." His words surprised her. "And her little lad."

"Ah! Little Bredon." She thought of the babe with genuine warmth. "You can imagine what a shock it was when she delivered a boy—the first male on the island for more than twenty years! Colleen has done well with him."

"I can see that, my dear," Bjorn said with a twinkle before his expression sobered once more. "Despite my fear, I have seen what life can bring forth, even amid such pain. You were right, Mary Irmengard, Guardian of Adytum. Life is risk. We will risk together, you and I, and trust in what brought us to each other after all these years."

Irma reached up to frame his face in her palms. "Bjorn." Her eyes searched his again. "I see you. I know who you are as well, a man of honor, a protector who has known grief but never abandoned joy. I promise you that I will take the greatest care when any danger finds us. You may trust me, and I will trust you, too." She lifted up on her toes to press a hard kiss to his lips, sealing their pact.

When she pulled away, he cast a look around the main hall. "Now where is that bed again?"

Her laughter reverberated through the high-ceilinged room, but then she took another step back from him as she recalled the conversation she had so recently left with Sister Grace and Sister Alice.

His expression turned from mirth to puzzlement.

"I am afraid we must wait for that." She felt a pang

of true regret. At her pronouncement, Bjorn's expression turned to frank dismay.

Irma silenced him with a lifted palm.

"Since you trust me, in all ways," she said, "as I do you, I must tell you what is afoot." Bjorn's gaze sharpened.

Irma thought of the alternate plan the conspirator nuns had proposed. A plan to permit the men to stay on the island, but more than that, for them to join together, women and men, and to reforge their community. They would tear down walls to build new ones.

With sudden clarity, she saw that Bjorn had a part to play as well.

"You sing." She recalled the bawdy tune they had harmonized when they'd first entered this hall together.

Bjorn's brow creased in confusion. "Yes, I suppose—"

"Come with me." She turned abruptly to lead him out the main doors, past the site of their first skirmish—martial and amorous—and he followed.

As they strolled the grounds one last time before they would have to part, Irma told him what she needed him to do.

Though visibly reluctant to be separated from her, he agreed.

****

A wistful melody drew Bjorn back to the main hall after his conversation with Irma. Notes of haunting sweetness tugged at him as they trailed through the air, leaving poignant, ghostly echoes in their wake. Following their cadence, he found himself face to face again with Andor. Remembering that he'd last seen the other man on the cliff path, setting off to find his lady love, Bjorn approached him.

"Haven't found your Frances yet?" After what he'd experienced with Irma, Bjorn found himself sympathetic to the other man's plight.

Though he didn't straighten from where he leaned against the wall, Andor lifted from his lips the brass horn Bjorn had seen him carrying through the forest. "I did find her," he replied.

"Ah," Bjorn said wisely. "Trouble there?" Bjorn was perversely relieved he wasn't the only one whose courtship had not proven easy.

"I don't know." His poet's mouth turned downward. "It's not her, though. It's these other nuns. They're making her do something, and I don't think it will be good for us."

The pieces began to fall together for Bjorn. "Your Frances, she's also a musician?"

Andor nodded and his eyes glazed over. "She makes the finest music man has ever heard. Music to lure the body, capture the heart, and soothe the spirit."

Bjorn coughed into his hand at that. "Is she the Sister Frances who leads the equinox ritual tomorrow?" He kept to his task instead of teasing the other man, so clearly lovesick as he was. By the goddess, Bjorn admitted honestly, he'd looked similarly as foolish as that this long day.

Andor finally straightened at Bjorn's question. "Yes, that's what they're making her do," he said. "What do you know of it?"

Thinking of what Irma had just told him, what she had asked him to arrange, Bjorn eyed the other man. "Andor, my friend," he said, "I have a use for your fine voice."

"My voice?" The other man's brow wrinkled in confusion.

"And do you know where we might get some more musical instruments?"

"We?" Bjorn saw understanding dawn in the other man's eyes. "You mean, we, the men in the band?"

"That I do," Bjorn confirmed.

"As it happens, I know where the instruments are. Frances told me to—that is, she gave me some instructions." Andor eyed Bjorn as if sizing him up as an ally.

"I'll bet she did." Bjorn smiled broadly, draping his arm over the other man's shoulders. "These nuns think of everything. Now show me where the instruments may be found."

Allowing Andor to lead him forward, Bjorn nevertheless paused just before they left the main hall to study the small chess board arranged in the corner.

"It's the set I carved for you!" Andor's voice rang out in the large room.

"It is indeed." Bjorn distractedly scratched at his beard.

"Someone's set up a game with it."

"A game I intend to win," Bjorn murmured, more to himself than to the man beside him.

With a thoughtful look at the arranged pieces, Bjorn moved one forward.

It was not the first time he had done so.

Chapter 17

Though Irma was usually among the leaders on the island, she also knew how to follow. For the last two days, the women of the island had rehearsed the *ceolchoirm*, the equinox ritual, under Sister Frances's capable direction.

They performed this ritual every year at the point when day and night were exactly equal, to celebrate the balance of nature—the balance of opposites—in the creation of the new life of spring.

This year, the ritual would be different.

Frances, Alice, Grace, and Catherine all had a hand in small changes here and there that would, they hoped, shape the ritual into …more …than what it had been.

Though they'd had to remain separate from their men this day, Irma knew that the men had been given their parts to play as well.

They would see if it was enough.

Now Irma sat in the second row of nuns in the Music Chamber as the last of the afternoon sun filtered in through the high windows. The women in these first two rows would sing the song of spring, the call to the goddess. Irma would joyfully lift her contralto to the cause.

The room fairly vibrated with expectation. In the rows behind Irma stood more nuns who would chant from the Sacred Scripts as directed, and they were all of them ringed by another group of nuns standing along the walls of the Music Chamber, who would play instrumental accompaniment on their harps, horns, and flutes.

From a chair in the corner of the dais, Mother Agnes presided over the ritual as she always did. Irma surveyed Agnes's determined expression and wondered what the other woman was thinking, how she would react to the changes wrought in the ritual.

Anticipation surged through Irma as Sister Frances lifted her hands and the chanting began, breaking the expectant silence of the room. Irma's part came soon after. She sang in full voice from her very core, letting soar her dreams—for herself and Bjorn, for all the women of the island …and all the men who had arrived here, as well.

Irma could tell when Mother Agnes sensed the ritual shift, when Sister Catherine's traditional call to the goddess was echoed by Sister Alice, who broke from tradition to issue a call to the masculine spirit of the island, a spirit previously dormant whom they called to rouse himself, to join together masculine and feminine in the cause of burgeoning life.

Mother Agnes stirred uneasily on her chair, making as if to rise.

But then, Irma's heart filled as she heard the answering voices of the barbarians, first coming from outside the convent walls, then from within the Music Chamber itself as the men invaded the ritual space with their own song of transformation and renewal. The two sets of voices, male and female, entwined in graceful harmony. Some men played instruments as well, Irma noted with approval. Soon the room filled with the powerful call to the goddess …and the god.

Though Irma kept singing, she could not help but search the men pouring in the windows and doorways for her own man, her bear, Yrse's Bjorn. Bear would join bear in this ritual today. As the music reached a climactic pitch, Irma knew her walls had fallen completely, as the Oracle had urged. Her heart was soft, and her spirit soared with the powerful music around them.

And then she saw him.

Their eyes met as Bjorn climbed boldly through a window, and Irma thought she could hear the rumbling bass of his voice. Other men streamed in behind him, but she did not see them. She saw only him. She tuned her harmony to his, heard the beauty of their song within the song of their community, the song of the island itself.

The music lifted them higher and higher, he singing to her, she to him, until with one final move of Frances's hands, they all fell, quite suddenly, silent.

Irma held her breath in that silence, as they all seemed to do collectively.

Waiting, through first one heartbeat, then another.

And then Bjorn exhaled on a loud whoop and threw himself into the crowd between them, pushing his way toward Irma. His battle cry threw the room into chaos as everyone raced toward others in the room.

Her eyes full of the man she loved, Irma forgot about Agnes and what the Mother Superior must be thinking about the ritual's outcome. For it was evident: the masculine spirit of the island had been roused indeed. Even Irma, pragmatic as she was, had felt the ritual's undeniable, transformative power. She could feel the god's presence, feel it entwining with that of the goddess herself. *Together. Together.*

Bjorn caught Irma up in his arms, bent his head to hers and sealed their reunion with a lusty kiss. Irma strained against him, climbing up his thick body like a monkey, wrapping her strong thighs around his. Without breaking the kiss, Bjorn walked forward with her, heading for the door that led out of the Music Chamber and into the Abbey's main hall.

"Aren't—you," Irma said between open-mouthed kisses, "—going—to look—where—you're going?"

"No—need," he returned. But he paused just outside the doorway, bracing her against the wall, slanting his mouth against hers, and stealing her senses. When he lifted his lips from hers again, he murmured against them, "I know where I'm going." Turning them again toward the staircase, his eyes crinkled at the corners just before he lifted his head and shouted to the ceiling, "A bed for my bride!"

"A bed for my groom!" Irma cried out in return, twining her arms around his neck and resting her smooth cheek against his bearded one.

They had come full circle. The battle was coming to its rightful conclusion.

The thought reminded her, and as he made for the stairs, other nuns and barbarians streaming around them, she tapped his shoulder with her palm. "Wait! Wait, Bjorn!"

He looked a question at her.

"Over there," she directed him. "I have to see …"

Understanding lit Bjorn's eyes.

Without another word, he carted her over to the corner of the main hall in which her chess match was being waged.

They surveyed the game together.

"Someone's moved another of my pieces!" Irma touched a white knight who had captured one of the black pieces. A frown creased Irma's brow. "Well, it's put me in a better position, but the game is still not finished," she grumbled.

"He seems to have gotten out of where you had him pinned."

"He—who do you mean?" Irma turned quickly to look into his eyes.

"Whoever we're playing against, my dear," he said, as if it were entirely obvious.

"Whoever *we're*—" She gaped at him. "I thought I was playing against you!"

"Against me!" he roared in outrage. "I would never wage war against you, my queen. I am your loyal knight." Removing a hand from where it cupped her bottom, Bjorn lifted the white piece she'd just touched. She could see that someone had carved it to have a bear-like face. "That's you?"

"Didn't you recognize me?" he teased. He set the piece back down carefully in the same place. "Who do you think has been helping you win this war?"

Irma sat back in his arms and looked at him. "Of course, you have." A slow grin curved her lips. "My white knight." She bestowed on him a soft, reverent kiss.

"And you are my queen, my Sigyn." Bjorn captured her mouth more boldly with his.

A delightfully long moment later, Irma regained the presence of mind to say, "Why do you call me Sigyn?"

"Sigyn, lass, is Loki's queen." He nuzzled her cheek. "Though Loki often did not deserve it, his Sigyn was always there for him," he explained carefully, "protecting him …even with her own body."

Irma heard what he was saying and tightened her arms around him.

"And …" Bjorn pulled back so that his moss-green eyes met hers. "Her name means Giver of Victory."

Irma frowned down at the unfinished game. "Well, I haven't done that yet." She thought of the match she played against an unknown opponent.

"Maybe not there," he admitted. "But you, Mary Irmengard, Guardian of Adytum and, if the goddess wills it, future mother of my children, have brought me the greatest triumph of my life."

Irma smiled up at him, feeling in this moment the glory of victory in truth.

"To life!" she shouted to the rafters.

"To life," he murmured to her, gazing at her with love and hope.

"Aye, then." She leaned into him to press her lips to the pulse in his neck, feeling the indication of vital forces that beat within him. "Let us celebrate."

Meeting his eyes again, she waggled her eyebrows. With a jubilant whoop, Bjorn hoisted her up and walked her backward to the stairs that led to her bedchamber, where they would complete their union.

And, Irma hoped, where they would plant the seeds of the new life that lay before them.

They would do so together—with trust, with passion, and with a love deeper than any she had ever known.

A love without disguises, without games, without walls.

A love without fear.

She felt like Sigyn indeed.

Victory would be theirs.

Main Characters and Terms

The Nuns of Adytum Abbey:

Sister Frances Ignatius (Andor): musician at the Abbey, has been there for seven years, leads the island's most important rituals

Sister Mary Irmengard/Irma (Bjorn): the Guardian General of Adytum, she has been the martial force protecting the island for fifteen years; she most often finds the new women who have arrived and brings them to the convent

Sister Catherine of the Oracle: the prophetess of the convent, connected with the magical feminine being who controls the island; she has been there for eighteen years

Mother Agnes of the Holy Water: the Mother Superior and leader of the convent, she founded the community twenty years before when she arrived with her small daughter, Angelina

Sister Benita: the Abbey's chef, presides over the dining hall, has been on the island for twenty years, arrived shortly after Agnes

Sister Angelina (Njal and Bo): as a baby came to the island twenty years ago with her mother, Agnes, and has no memories of life before the island; she oversees the gardens and attends those in the sick ward

Sister Grace (Ivar): Frances's roommate, very shy, assists in the Abbey Library by teaching new arrivals to read the sacred texts; she has been on the island for five years

Sister Alice (Magnus): Keeper of the Sacred Scripts, archivist and chief librarian of the Abbey, she protects and adds to the most important documents of the Library; she has been on the island for thirteen years

Sister Colleen: Adytum's dairy maid; she has a small child, Bredon, to whom she gave birth on the island shortly after she arrived about a year before

Sisters Veronique and Agatha: best friends and Abbey guardians, they are skilled in archery; they have been on the island for four years

Astrid: the latest woman to arrive on the island, unconscious

Barbarians:

Andor (Frances): bard of the barbarian fleet, a musician and expert bone and wood-carver, the soul of an artist

Trygve: loyal friend of Andor, steadfast and humble

Skade: impulsive, the youngest member of the barbarian band; this is his first raid

Bjorn (Mary Irmengard): a bear-like man, jovial and martial

Njal (Angelina): a giant of a man, gruff and cautious; he is best friends with Bo, with whom he shares everything

Bo (Angelina): more compactly built than other barbarians; he is mischievous and ingenious

Frode: mysterious and strategic; he has a shrewd intelligence that has led him to a place of prominence in the barbarian band

Magnus (Alice): Harald's brother, a berserker who can be provoked to violent rage

Ivar (Grace): an older man and former treasure hunter, friend of Harald's family

Harald: half-crazed leader of the barbarian invasion; he has come to the island on a desperate quest

Terms:

bacraut: asshole
brúðr: bride
ceolchoirm: Irish word referring to a concert or festival; on the island it refers specifically to the spring equinox ritual
kuensami: skirt-chaser
lodinkinni: person with shaggy hair
saeta: sweetheart
vitskirtr: lack-wit

Mythical People, Places, and Things:

Asgard: dwelling place of the gods in Norse mythology

Baldr: a beloved god who represents daylight and courage in Norse mythology

Freya: goddess of love and fertility (among many other things), legend has it that she wears a feathered coat and has a chariot drawn by cats

Gungnir: Odin's spear

Idunn: a fertility goddess in Norse mythology; her apples provided eternal youth to the gods

Jotun: a race of evil giants in Norse myth

Loki: a shape-changing trickster among the Norse gods

Mimir: water-spirit known for wisdom and foresight, may have possessed a tree that contained Odin's eye, affording him predictive powers; after he was beheaded, Odin carried his head with him

Nine Realms: according to Norse mythology, the universe is divided into nine different worlds

Nine Nights: Odin hanged himself on the tree of life (Yggdrasil) for nine nights in order to gain insights into other worlds

Odin: god of war and wisdom, protector of heroes

Sigyn: Loki's wife, she collected a serpent's venom in a bowl so that it would not drip on him; when she paused to empty the bowl, he felt the venom at last, and his pain created earthquakes

Thor: a Norse god associated with storms and fertility, known for wielding a hammer

Valkyries: women who served Odin in Valhalla and chose the worthy among dead warriors to take their place there in the afterlife

Dear Readers,

As I hope will be obvious, the characters you encounter in these stories are neither nuns nor barbarians in any sort of real, historical sense.

You may wonder, when is this story set? And where? And what nationality are all these characters? As at least one minor side character Scot says in every Highlander romance: "*Dinna fash yerself!*"

This series is intentionally unspecific, a collage—even, if you will, a pastiche. Just enjoy and let the anachronistic and borderless references wash over you, bringing whatever images, settings, accents, and technologies to mind that you will.

The story's purpose is to delight, amuse, arouse, and perhaps make you sigh a little in the end knowing that love conquers all, including some very much not-Catholic nuns and these Viking-like but technically unspecified barbarians.

It's all just for fun. I hope you enjoyed it.

Wishing you love,
Kay

A word about the author...

Kay Jeffery is a professional historian who loves stories. One day during her midlife crisis, Kay remembered that she'd always wanted to write romance novels. Her husband said, "I think you should do it." Her kids were glad to have her (more or less) out of their business. Thrilled to have a stable lap for long periods of time, the cats discovered quickly that typing does not preclude scritches. And so, Kay carved out pockets of time in between family life and work to research such arcana as medieval musical instruments, Norse swear words, ancient Celtic rituals, obscure mythological divinities—and to weave them all together. Her writing builds a fantasy world where intelligent, loyal, and courageous heroines and heroes find their way to each other, where dreams are realized, and where love always, always wins. kayjeffery.com

Thank you for purchasing
this publication of The Wild Rose Press, Inc.

For questions or more information
contact us at
info@thewildrosepress.com.

The Wild Rose Press, Inc.
www.thewildrosepress.com